COMMENTS

This novel takes the reader on a journey from before the dawn of time until the end of days. Prepare to question your doubts and challenge your faith. Courage is waiting.
—Kary Oberbrunner, Author of Elixir Project and Your Secret Name

WOW! This is such an incredible story. I love the way Josh's PTSD is represented. It is scary but this story could so easily become reality. The ending gave me goose-bumps. I am on the edge of my seat with anticipation. So many unanswered questions. I love it.
—Lorie Gurnett, Author of The Kingdom Series

There's low art and high art. This book is high art. Low art is solely for entertainment.
—Deborah Stewart, Retired Transition House Director for women and children fleeing domestic violence

MANHUNT reminds me of *The Zion Chronicles*. I could scarcely put those books down. The authors Bodie and Brock Thoene thanked Rena for her high words of praise and the high honor of thinking an endorsement form them would be significant. Unfortunately, they couldn't comment on her book as they are currently writing their own similar book so couldn't risk reading her book and copying her ideas. To read this story is to encounter a world that was — and an apocalyptic world that could be. I highly recommend it. The book is life-changing.
—Dr. Hendrik Jan Groot BCM, MDiv, DMin

I believe you were anointed and inspired by the Holy Spirit to write this. It's an up-to-date relevant message for the time we are in. I believe God will use this book to awaken those who read it.
—Jillian Armit, Retired Support and Education Coordinator Alzheimer Society of BC Upper Fraser Valley

Follow Josh in both his personal inner struggles as a believer and as a soldier afflicted with PTSD as he is being hunted down in a post-Christian apocalyptic world while worrying about his beloved, captured family. *MANHUNT* is a novel for readers who enjoy eschatology (the study of end times) with a bold, prophetic message for the Western church.

— Bill Oord
Philosopher and Theologian

WOW! WOW! WOW! That is how I would describe MANHUNT. It was such a gripping story I couldn't put it down. The words rang so true it made me sit back and re-evaluate not only my relationship with God but also my relationships with those around me. When you first start the book you need to readjust your focus and pay very close attention to the words. Words so powerful you don't remember reading them many times before. We live in a fallen and broken world and this story is a good glimpse at how fast life can change. How as Christians we are persecuted for spreading The Word of God. How evil lurks around every corner, waiting to destroy us. Josh does such an amazing job of walking us through the story, allowing us to enter into his world. I could feel his pain and frustration, his lack of faith and his turn around in life. I felt like I was following right beside him on his journey.
I can't wait for the next book in this amazing trilogy.

— Betty Vander Wier
Beloved daughter of the Most High God

MANHUNT

ONLY THE STRONG SURVIVE

Trust God ♡!
He loves you more
than you could
ever imagine! ♡

Rena Groot

AUTHOR ACADEMY elite

Rena ♡ Groot

MANHUNT, *Only the Strong Survive*

The Narrow Path Trilogy, Book 1

© 2020 by Rena Groot. All rights reserved.

Printed in the United States of America

Published by Author Academy Elite

PO Box 43, Powell, OH 43065
www.AuthorAcademyElite.com

All rights reserved. This book contains material protected under International and Federal Copyright Laws and Treaties. Any unauthorized reprint or use of this material is prohibited. No part of this book may be reproduced or transmitted in any form or by any means, electronic or mechanical, including photocopying, recording, or by any information storage and retrieval system, without express permission from the author.

Library of Congress Control Number: 2020910745

ISBN
Paperback: 978-1-64746-327-4
Hardback: 978-1-64746-328-1
E-book: 978-1-64746-329-8

Available in paperback, hardback, e-book, and audiobook.

All Scripture quotations are taken from the World English Bible (WEB), Public Domain.

Book design by Jetlaunch.net
Cover Design by Debbie O'Byrne — Debbie@JetLaunch.net

Edited in collaboration with
Deborah J. Stewart, Debra Sonnichsen and Inez Mitchell

WARNING

God spoke this warning thousands of years ago…

*"But if the watchman sees the sword come,
and doesn't blow the trumpet,
and the people aren't warned,
and the sword comes,
and takes any person from among them;
he is taken away in his iniquity,
but his blood I will require at the watchman's hand."
Ezekiel 33:6*

The Narrow Path Trilogy is a warning.
I pray you hear the warning and flee
from the wrath to come.

DEDICATION

This book is dedicated to my forever King,
the LORD Jesus Christ.
I am so thankful You are love incarnate.

―⁂―

This book is also dedicated to you, dear reader.
May you trust God,
walk in courage, truth and love,
and stay far from deception.

"For many deceivers have gone out into the world..."
2 John 1:7

Contents

The Rebellion 1

Manhunt 11

Broken Dreams 23

Rachel 35

News 51

Where Were You, God? 67

The Pit 75

Sweet Home Alabama 89

The Witnesses 109

The Children's Prison 123

Sheep Among Wolves 137

Love Not Your Life Unto Death 145

Released 153

Deep Darkness 171

Betrayal 181

About the Author 191

Photo Credits 193

The Rebellion

"...I saw Satan having fallen like lightning from Heaven."
Luke 10:18

MANHUNT

The sons of God sat in council among the ancient mists in the high courts of Heaven. Shockingly, an angel arose and declared he would be like the Most High. Proudly announcing his throne would be higher than God's — breathing rebellion — Lucifer invited other sons of God to follow.

He forgot something vitally important.

He was not God.

Adorned with every precious stone at his creation — musical pipes were infused into his innermost being. Music flowed from him with every breath. Lucifer, the "Light Bearer", led worship to God Almighty. He was the seal of perfection — full of wisdom and perfect in beauty — the anointed, guardian cherub over the throne of God. He had been on the holy mountain and walked in the midst of the stones of fire. No other angel had a more exalted position of honor in the heavenly realms.

That elevated position was not enough.

He wanted more.

Blinded by pride, Lucifer couldn't see he could never be greater than God. Myriads of angels stood with him. The rebellion started a war in Heaven.

Filled with violence — Lucifer was cast as a disgraceful thing from the holy mountain of God — expelled from the stones of fire. The rebellion was smashed and judgment pronounced. Lucifer's name was changed to Satan, the Accuser or Adversary. All who chose to follow him were cast out of Heaven.

"How you have fallen from Heaven,
shining one, son of the dawn!
How you are cut down to the ground,
who laid the nations low!
You said in your heart, "I will ascend into Heaven!
I will exalt my throne above the stars of God!
I will sit on the mountain of assembly, in the far north!
I will ascend above the heights of the clouds!
I will make myself like the Most High!"
Isaiah 14:12-14

God Almighty — the fulness of love, compassion, truth, beauty, purity, and holiness — dwells in realms of unspeakably glorious light. There is no darkness in Him at all. Righteousness and truth are the foundation of His throne. Love and faithfulness go before Him.

By choosing rebellion, Lucifer abandoned everything God is. Satan's domain became one of darkness and depravity. He can appear as an angel of light — perhaps transforming into a shadow of the glorious beauty he once had in Heaven. Behind the appearance of light and beauty is unimaginable evil.

Enraged his plans to rule the Kingdom of Heaven were thwarted, Satan must have longed for vengeance — to grieve God's heart and cause Him pain.

Leading man into ruin and rebellion would be the perfect plan. Satan must have anxiously waited for his opportunity to steal, kill and destroy God's precious creation.

Finally, his chance arrived — Eve walked alone in the garden of God. If Satan could get the woman to doubt God's Word, the innocence of Eden would be lost. Would the woman defy God? Would she eat what God told Adam not to eat?

Satan must have had his fingers crossed that day. Everything rested on Eve's decision to disobey God and choose her own path. He had deceived one-third of the angels who had stood in the presence of God — so maybe he thought his plan was foolproof? A small lie — a small disobedience — and Paradise would be lost. Mankind would be doomed to eternity in Hell with the father of lies.

Perhaps it was early morning. The garden must have pulsated with life and beauty — flawless — pure and exquisite. Maybe shafts of pure light streamed through the trees. Possibly dewdrops sparkled like tiny diamonds on every leaf. Perfume from myriads of flowers must have been heavy in the air.

Who knew what dark horror lay hidden amongst all this loveliness? Coiled in the tree of the knowledge of good and evil, Satan waited for his prey.

Why wasn't Eve alarmed to meet a talking serpent? Was there something hypnotic in his eyes? Did this talking creature, seductively casting doubt on God's Word, fascinate her? Was she enamored with the beauty of his glistening jewels? Perhaps he breathed music as he spoke. That would have been so mesmerizing as Eve had probably never heard music before. Did his words sound like truth?

Perhaps the conversation sounded like this...

"Hey beautiful. Eve. Psst. Over here."

(That's right. Let my beauty dazzle you. I am incredibly gorgeous, aren't I?)

"Has God really said you must not eat the fruit from every tree of the garden?"

"No. We can eat from all the trees. There's only one God said not to eat or touch."

(God didn't actually say don't touch it, Eve. You've embellished the instructions. That's great, Eve. I'm so proud of you.)

"Naw. You won't die."

"Really?"

"Yes. Your eyes will be opened and you will become like God." *(Yeah. That's the story. Are you buying it, Eve?)*

"But God said…"

"Look at how beautiful it is. Doesn't it look luscious? Go ahead. Pick it." *(What are you waiting for? Look at the fruit!)*

"One bite won't hurt."

"You're right. It glows like a jewel."

"Right? Didn't I tell you? So delightful. Can you imagine how delicious it must be?"

"But God…"

"God's holding out on you." (*Hurry it up, would you? I haven't got all day!*) "You will be like God, Eve."

"But…"

"You will know good and evil. Trust me."

Eve didn't see the trap. She didn't realize it was a huge deception that would enslave mankind for all of human history. How could she possibly have known? How Satan must have laughed as Eve took her first bite.

Eve gave the fruit to Adam and he ate. They satisfied the lust of the flesh (eating the forbidden fruit) — the lust of the eyes (it looked so tempting) — and the pride of life (you will be like God). Eve was deceived into thinking she could make her own decision and become her own God. She didn't realize the penalty was death.

> *"For the wages of sin is death,*
> *but the free gift of God is eternal life*
> *in Christ Jesus our Lord."*
> *Romans 6:23*

She invited Adam to join in her transgression. He walked in fully knowing he was choosing Eve over God. They committed high treason against the Lord of Life and rejected the relationship He offered. If only they had trusted God.

Once bathed in innocence — man now embraced Satan's rebellion and depravity. He must have been ecstatic. God's beautiful earth would come under his dominion. How his laughter must have reverberated throughout the canyons of Hell. The Prince of Darkness became the god of this world.

> *"Even if our Good News is veiled, it is*
> *veiled in those who are dying,*
> *in whom the god of this world has blinded*
> *the minds of the unbelieving,*
> *that the light of the Good News of the glory of Christ,*
> *who is the image of God, should not dawn on them."*
> *2 Corinthians 4:3-4*

MANHUNT

Don't be too quick to judge Adam and Eve. How many times have we believed the lies and walked into the snares?

"For all have sinned, and fall short of the glory of God."
Romans 3:23

God promised one day the head of the serpent would be crushed by the seed of the woman. One day the beauty of earth would be restored. One glorious day Messiah would rule and reign in righteousness with all who chose to follow Him.

That was the time of the beginning.

Now is the time of the end.

The children of Satan walk among the children of God. Who are they? You must be wise to discern. By their fruit you will know them. There are many wolves in the midst of the sheep. As it was in the days of Noah, when men's hearts were evil continuously, so it is for many today.

"For they don't sleep unless they do evil.
Their sleep is taken away, unless they make someone fall."
Proverbs 4:16

Earth has been divided into ten quadrants for several years now. Thousands of years before you took your first breath an ancient Book said this would happen. These divisions are represented by ten toes of iron mixed with clay. The people of the end are a mixture of thoughts, beliefs, cultures, languages, and religions. Although attempts have been made to create a one-world government and a one-world religion all could embrace, no unity will ever exist in this kingdom. This is earth's final kingdom — partially strong as iron — partially weak as clay.

Revolutions, rebellions, anarchy, and global disasters are being displayed on earth's stage such as the world has never seen. A kingdom of chaos.

RENA GROOT

"Unless those days had been shortened,
no flesh would have been saved.
But for the sake of the chosen ones,
those days will be shortened."
Matthew 24:22

One day, God will grind this kingdom to powder.
It will blow away like dust in the wind.
If you are reading this, it is the time of man's final kingdom.
It is a time of transition and great global upheaval.
One day —
maybe soon —
Jesus the Messiah will rule and reign in His eternal
Kingdom.
But not yet.
There is more to come.
The ancient, narrow path is calling.
Only the strong survive.
Come…

PART 1

MANHUNT

Manhunt

*"Behold, I will send for many fishermen," says Yahweh,
"and they will fish them up. Afterward
I will send for many hunters,
and they will hunt them from every
mountain, from every hill,
and out of the clefts of the rocks."
Jeremiah 16:16*

MANHUNT

Josh struggled to catch his breath. Looking for a way to escape — he realized with horror things would never be the same. The street he knew like the back of his hand seemed unfamiliar — as if he'd never been there before.

The drones flying overhead appeared unusually interested in him. The whirring sounds were unnerving. What if he was picked up on facial recognition?

He had to get away. Was any place safe?

Was it only moments before he had walked down Montgomery Avenue to catch the news at Frederickson's Appliances? The shop was so familiar. Pa told him he had gone there as a boy back in the 1940's.

Was it only a month ago he and his buddy Tom had taken their TV's out to the field behind Tom's barn and let loose with their rifles? It surprised them how easily a 22 could shatter two fifty-two-inch screens. It seemed like a great idea at the time. Many of the TV programs were so vile they didn't want their family's watching them. To see the news now, Josh had to stand outside the store window watching the displayed TV.

All news disappeared on the Internet. Blocked. It was scrubbed clean of anything that smacked of rebellion. There was only approved information about the goings on in the ten earth quadrants.

The shop was an easy two-mile walk from his house. The exercise a couple times a week was needed because of Rachel's good cooking. Josh enjoyed the crisp air and the sound of leaves crunching beneath his feet. Thankfully, he had worn his favorite wool hat. It seemed way too early for summer to be over, but the gold, orange, and scarlet of the tulip poplars and oaks lining the street clearly announced the season. It would be dark soon. He had to hurry. There was just enough time to visit Frederickson's and be back home in time to hug his little Juliet goodnight.

Walking past the same windows he peered into since childhood, Josh shivered. He had a sense something terrible was about to happen. He tried to shake off the feelings but they'd somehow latched onto his heart.

Old Mr. Riley sat in his creaking rocking chair on the front porch of his store, providing a genuine comfort in that simple act. He'd sat rocking and whittling in that chair since as far back as Josh could remember.

"Evenin' Josh. Crops harvested yet?"

Was there an edge in his voice?

The old man seemed as if he was trying to sound casual but it didn't quite come out that way. Mr. Riley looked at Josh as if he was a stranger — as if he hadn't known him his whole life. Strange. Glancing around, Josh tried to figure out what was wrong. The same shops lined the street. He could see nothing unusual. Frederickson's still stood across from The Rock. Josh liked to take his little family there for chai lattes and chocolate sparks — Rachel's favorite. Why did he feel so apprehensive?

A smoky smell in the air reminded him of campfires as a boy — roasting marshmallows — chasing fireflies. Dogs barked in the distance. It all seemed so normal yet somehow it wasn't.

Josh cleared his throat before answering the gentleman. He hoped to sound as if he didn't suspect anything unusual.

"Hey, Mr. Riley. Yes, sir. Got most of my crops harvested. Rachel and I picked all the pecans and cabbages. The corn's almost ready. Just a few bush beans and mustard greens left."

They had been having such crazy weather. He thanked God most of his crops survived, in spite of the drought, tornados, and insects. Lightning storms started dry crops on fire. The fact that there were two "prophets" in Jerusalem who seemed to have authority to stop the rain, didn't help. He knew it was prophesied this would happen in the ancient Book. Knowing that didn't make it easier. Water had to be pumped from the river for irrigation. It was a hardship for folks who didn't have access to the river. Earlier in the season bollworms and spider mites attacked the cotton — ending that harvest. Josh didn't want to think about the cotton. Thankfully he'd only planted a few acres.

Mr. Riley didn't reply — just kept rocking and staring. Quite unnerving. Mr. Riley almost always had something to say. Calling out a hasty goodbye, Josh felt eyes following him as he

MANHUNT

walked away.

That was very strange.

Except for Mr. Riley, the street was deserted. That was odd. Normally people would be hanging around the storefronts — chatting about the crops — the crazy weather. Things had changed a lot recently. Folks kept to themselves more — weren't as friendly. The street looked tired, dusty, and old. Trees provided the only real beauty.

The heaviness in the air since the news reminded him things change — things the Bible said would happen one day. Had that day arrived?

He hurried towards the window, trying to shrug off the apprehension. Even though the closed sign hung on the door, one TV in the window played on through the night.

The word "MANHUNT" flashed across the screen in large, neon red letters. Not the news he hoped to see. There seemed to be someone new being hunted every day. The so-called enemies of the state increased daily.

This announcement took his breath away.

A name rolled across the screen.

His throat went dry and his stomach convulsed. He thought anyone standing close would have heard his heart pounding against his ribs.

Three bars under a name indicated the person was a wanted, dangerous criminal. This name had three bars.

His name.

Josh had a habit of speaking aloud when he felt stressed. He was stressed now.

"What on earth? Maybe someone with the same name?"

A photo flashed above the name.

His face — his name!

Joshua Williams.

"What? There must be a mistake — a horrible mistake. They've mixed me up with someone else."

Something blocked his throat and impeded his breath. Hard as he tried — gasping for air — he couldn't fill his lungs.

Where could he go? The police would never believe there'd been a mistake. They'd throw him in jail in a heartbeat — standard operating procedure these days. A man was considered guilty until proven innocent.

"Think, Josh! Think!"

He couldn't go home because the Manhunters would likely be waiting there.

The announcer continued.

Josh tried to focus on the screen while willing himself to breathe slowly. His Post Traumatic Stress Disorder — PTSD — counseling came back to him.

"Stay calm. Breathe."

Though he couldn't hear through the store window, he could read the announcer's lips.

"A reward of three thousand dollars will be paid for the capture of this criminal. This is the second announcement."

"Three thousand dollars? Second announcement?"

His world shifted in an instant.

"Was that why Mr. Riley acted so strange?"

Josh hurried away. Even though he couldn't hear her voice, Josh imagined the TV announcer screaming, *"There he is! Get him!"*

Like lightning — snippets of his life — everything he'd ever done wrong — played like an automatic weapon pelting him — one sin after another.

"But I haven't done anything worthy of a manhunt. I've never committed a real crime."

His past PTSD made his mind wander when the anxiety was too great. His mind responded to shock by momentarily blanking out — his way of coping — of not being overwhelmed. He was now blissfully unaware of the news he saw. His mind drifted. Long ago he chose to abide by the law and stay out of trouble.

"I just want to live a simple life — love my family — farm my land. No harm in that."

MANHUNT

Pa had given him a third of a section of land on what he considered the most magnificent property on earth — an area known as the Shoals — just outside of Sheffield, Alabama. Thinking of his home on the banks of the Tennessee River made him smile.

"This coming year looks like it should be a good one."

This would be the first time he had enough money to take his family on a holiday. Thoughts of Rachel and Juliet caused his heart to thump faster as his mind snapped back to the present.

"Are they safe? What will happen to them?"

Brushing fears aside — trying to think calming thoughts — Josh scolded himself.

"Smarten up, Josh. Panicking won't help."

He had to get out of Sheffield — but he couldn't go home.

"Now what???"

His heart was racing. Josh took off taking long strides.

"Easy, Josh. Slow down. Drawing any attention might be fatal."

His racing heart settled as he made himself slow his pace.

"Calm down, Josh. You'll figure this out."

The howling dogs sounded closer. Were they hunting for him? If the Manhunters had dogs on his trail he had to get to the river — fast! It was less than a quarter of a mile to the Tennessee River. His only hope was to make it there without being seen.

Josh broke into a cold sweat as he saw Earl walking towards him. Earl wanted to buy his land, but Josh would never break his promise to Pa and sell the land. Had Earl heard the news? Josh had to pretend everything was normal.

"Hey there, Earl. How are you?"

The man didn't seem like his friendly self. Something was wrong.

Glancing behind, Mr. Riley was still rocking and staring on his porch. He looked like a cat that had just swallowed a canary.

"I'm fine, Josh. How 'bout you? Didn't you sleep last night? You look terrible."

Did Earl's eyes narrow when he asked that or did he only squint into the setting sun?

"Fine, Earl. It's been a long day. Just heading home."

"Walking? Wait a minute. I'll give you a ride."

He seemed too eager to give Josh a ride. Josh's throat tightened and his heart pounded.

"Thanks Earl, but I need exercise — been eating too much of Rachel's cornbread."

Josh tried to laugh but it came out forced — kind of nervous sounding.

"See you around, Earl."

Trying to walk calmly away, Josh was thankful the road to the river was the same way to his house. Earl would get suspicious if he started walking in a different direction. When he was out of earshot Josh muttered to himself,

"This can't be happening. What do they think I've done?"

His evaluation card was stellar — top scores — taxes paid on time — animals and garden produce shipped to the government as required. He never spoke negatively about the king.

Rumors had spread about a selection. Had he been selected for the Territories where he'd be let loose among the beasts?

"The Territories? That means death. Once those gates close, there's no coming back."

He shouldn't have been sentenced to the guillotine for population control or rebellion. His age should save him from that fate.

"They usually only select the old folks — fifty or older."

When stressed, flashbacks of the horror of Afghanistan played like a video across his mind. The PTSD pulled him back to the sounds of guns firing — bullets whirring — moans and screams filled his ears.

"Don't go there. Easy, Josh. Calm down."

His head reeled as he made himself look at the present reality. For the reward offered for criminals many turned in family and friends. It proved enough of a temptation to make a man betray another. Tom came to mind — the closest to a blood brother he had — friends since childhood.

"Can I trust Tom? Is our friendship enough? Would I be safe at his farm?"

MANHUNT

He turned his ear towards the mournful wailing of the bloodhounds and held his breath. It seemed the hounds were moving in his direction. They could smell prey long before they saw it.

"Could be they're only chasing a coon."

He pulled his hat further down and kept moving.

The river wound past his place — if he followed it — he could at least see about his family. If the dogs were after him, once in the water they would lose his scent and the trail would go cold.

Alligators used to stay in the coastal waters of the Mobile Delta. Lately they'd moved into the Tennessee and Elk Rivers. Still, what choice did he have? How else could he lose the mongrels and the Manhunters? Hopefully it was too far north for any gators to be around. The cold Alabama winters usually kept the gator population down — but it wasn't winter.

Time seemed to stand still as darkness descended. Once under cover of the two-hundred-year-old oaks Josh ran full out towards the river. He had to avoid the bluff walls. If anyone fell over the bluffs they likely wouldn't survive the drop. There was a big ol' black walnut within a few yards of the bluff. Pa once told him that tree was used as a shelter when Andrew Jackson and his men camped there. They were on their way to the battle of New Orleans back in 1812. The ancient giant marked the place where he had to veer left to avoid the bluffs.

A sudden movement caught his eye. A four-foot water moccasin startled him as it slithered towards the water. His heart beat faster. If he'd been closer to the venomous snake he might have stepped on it. He was thankful that reptile wasn't in an ornery mood.

Josh shivered as he slipped into the cold water. He was thankful for the new moon that held back its light and didn't betray his presence. Swishing sounds along the shore made him imagine a gator sliding into the water to meet him.

"Don't stress, Josh. You'll be fine..."

Stealth came second nature. He had been trained as a Marine to move covertly day or night. His special operations team was deployed to bring peace and order amidst the chaos of Afghanistan.

His work had been classified — even his parents didn't know what he did.

Josh thought about the Tennessee River — so much like the Kabul River that flowed from the Hindu Kush Mountains. It was three to forty feet deep — highly unpredictable — and varied in width from fifty to two hundred yards. Appearing calm on the surface — unseen dangers lurked in the depths. Hidden undertows could drag a man downstream. Once caught in the rapids a strong swimmer could easily drown.

Trying to keep as close as possible to shore so he wouldn't fall into one of the deep holes, Josh was disheartened to hear thunder rumble across the sky. He'd have to hurry to find shelter.

Concern for his wife and daughter quickened his pace as something swished by his leg.

"Probably not a gator. Probably just a big ol' catfish or a largemouth bass."

The lights around his house came into view. Relief flooded his heart. He could at least see if his girls were safe.

Josh felt swishing by his leg again — then a vice-like grip on his thigh. He barely had time to grab a breath before the gator pulled him under. It tried to drag him into deep water where it could plunge him into a death roll to drown him. Josh realized he didn't have much time. He fought with all his might — frantically searching for his pocketknife. His fingers wrapped around it. He flicked it open and jabbed repeatedly at the monster's snout — gouging at the gator's eye. It screamed in pain as it released its hold.

Josh swam hard for the surface. He desperately needed air. Making a frantic lunge for shore, he stumbled out of the water — climbing into the sheltering branches of a big ol' oak.

Too stressed and shocked to feel pain, Josh watched blood trickling down his thigh. The gator's teeth left deep puncture holes — hardly any slashing or tears. *"Thankfully, it doesn't look too bad — looks like the beast missed the main arteries."* Shredded pants were a small price to pay for freedom.

MANHUNT

Treed like a cornered animal — miserable, cold, wet, and wounded — Josh desperately wanted to talk to Rachel. She'd help him make sense of this madness. Maybe he could make a run for his house?

"Don't do it, Josh. It'd be insanity to try talk to her. It'd endanger her life."

Josh wondered why the world was such a mess. What part did the new technology play in all this? A few folks claimed technical glitches in the Artificial Intelligence AI Program caused malfunctions in the system. Solar flare interference was blamed for AIs breaking down. With them carrying out all government programs, this was a serious issue.

The AI system began randomly selecting names — sent out notices to the Manhunters that those folks were criminals. Sentenced to the Territories — people screamed of being falsely accused — but as they were hauled away people looked the other way. They had to. If folks tried to intervene they would be hauled away too.

"Had those people been innocent?"

He had no other options.

He had to ask Tom for help.

Well, maybe he could hide in Tom's hayloft and think a bit more about options...

Broken Dreams

*"Therefore I take pleasure in weaknesses,
in injuries, in necessities,
in persecutions, and in distresses, for Christ's sake.
For when I am weak, then am I strong."
2 Corinthians 12:10*

Pulling his jacket tighter, all Josh could think about was Rachel and Juliet. Were they okay? He had to let Rachel know this was all a terrible mistake — he'd figure it out — he hadn't done anything wrong.

Climbing down from the oak was hard — his leg's stiffness surprised him. Dropping to the ground Josh hid in the shadows. All was quiet. He could see the silhouettes of Rachel's sunflowers standing like soldiers beside the house. Everything looked peaceful — normal.

Josh crawled towards his house and froze. His sobbing little girl pleaded with a huge man not to take her away from her Mama and Daddy. The man snarled at her to shut up as he carried her to a black van.

"Daddy! Help me! Please, Daddy!" The cries pierced Josh's heart. He was about to jump up and make a run for his daughter when he saw the guns holstered to the man's side. Guards stood by with semi-automatic weapons. His heart broke as he realized he could do nothing to protect his little girl.

The van drove away with his precious daughter.

"God, where are they taking my Juliet? Please protect her."

Josh crept towards his house. Before he could look in the window to see if Rachel was okay, another van squealed down the driveway. Two huge men carried a body out of his house. An arm hung limply. He knew that arm. It was Rachel's.

He wanted to run and shout at the men to get away from his wife — to bring his daughter back — but he felt paralyzed — outnumbered. His chest tightened. He could barely breathe as he watched the van drive off with his beloved wife.

"Is she unconscious? Dead? Where are they taking her? Oh God, please keep her in Your care."

Numb from the cold and stress, Josh tried to stand. He groaned from the pain of the gator bite. His head throbbed. Perhaps this was all a nightmare. Maybe he would wake up soon and Juliet would be jumping on the bed to give him good morning hugs. Rachel would be in the kitchen making biscuits and gravy. Soon Juliet would be going to school on the little sawed-off bus that picked her up at the gate. The sunshine would be streaming through the windows and life would be normal and good.

Josh realized with dread this was not one of his frequent nightmares. He watched as the van turned towards the interstate highway. His heart went with the van.

Josh looked across the field at his animals. He could hear them crying for their supper.

Beauty's nose sniffed the wind as she whinnied — his spirited black Arab knew he was near. He longed to go to them, but armed guards had been strategically posted around his house. Feeding his animals was not going to happen.

"God, please take care of the animals."

Josh tried to come up with a plan — so difficult — his thoughts were so muddled. His leg hurt badly. It was way past the middle of the night. Shoving his hands into his pockets he turned his face away from the cold wind. He was determined to get his family back.

"But how?"

A neighbor's dog barking made him jump. He had to get to Tom's barn. If he could make it there without being seen, he could hide in the hayloft and sleep. At least he would be in a safe place for now. He hadn't decided yet if he could trust Tom. The sun would be coming up soon so he had no time to lose.
Josh dragged his legs over his field of ruined cotton. His hands were so stiff from the cold he could barely unhook the barn's door latch. As it creaked open, he ducked to get in the door. Being tall had its drawbacks. Josh was greeted by the cackling of startled hens. He winced as he covered his nose — the sharp stench of manure was overpowering.

Climbing into the hayloft, Josh buried himself in a huge mound of hay to make his body as inconspicuous as possible. Tom had left a radio droning in the barn. Josh was half asleep when he heard the radio announcer telling folks about another great earthquake.

"Another earthquake? Unbelievable."

MANHUNT

The announcer tried to sound calm but you could hear fear in her voice. She informed listeners this was an earthquake of epic proportions in Chile. It was the most powerful earthquake ever recorded with a magnitude of 9.8. Josh thought how one day there would be an earthquake like the world had never seen. Islands would be removed and mountains would fall into the heart of the sea. This current earthquake would seem like nothing, as people would cry for the rocks to fall on them to hide them from the wrath of God. *"How absurd to think they could hide from God,"* Josh murmured as he closed his eyes and fell into a deep, troubled sleep.

The morning light was blinding. The cackling chickens and crowing rooster confused Josh.

"Where am I? Why am I lying in a pile of hay?"

Memory slowly returned. Josh felt his leg to see if the fight with a gator had been a dream. It wasn't. Hay and dirt covered the gator bite. Realizing the wound had to be cleaned, Josh painfully climbed down from the loft to get water from the trough. He was so hungry the half-eaten apple on top of the pig's slop looked appealing.

With nowhere else to go, Josh climbed back into the loft. He peered through a crack in the wood siding towards his farm — armed guards still patrolled his yard. Josh thought about Rachel and Juliet. *"God, please look after them."*

He thought about his crazy, recurring dream. There was a long, loud trumpet blast — like a ram's horn — a shofar he once heard. People vanished. It reminded him of an old Star Trek re-run where people were dematerialized and beamed up into the clouds. Folks called it the Rapture — the strangest thing ever. He knew why he was left behind when the trumpet blasted. He'd decided long ago he didn't need God — could manage life just fine on his own. Rachel was independent and didn't need God either. They committed their lives to Christ soon after the

Rapture. Millions did. They hadn't believed the Bible was true until then. It was obvious to any thinking person what happened. Every single person who disappeared was a follower of Jesus Christ.

> *"For the Lord himself will descend*
> *from Heaven with a shout,*
> *with the voice of the archangel and with God's trumpet.*
> *The dead in Christ will rise first, then we who are alive,*
> *who are left, will be caught up together*
> *with them in the clouds,*
> *to meet the Lord in the air.*
> *So we will be with the Lord forever."*
> *1 Thessalonians 4:16-17*

Josh searched the Bible to see what was going to happen next. He was profoundly impacted as he studied God's Word — amazed how he understood many things that made no sense to him before.

"Why didn't I see the truth before? Why was I so foolish?"

Wishing he and Rachel had been ready when Jesus came for His own was pointless. The cares of life prevented them from listening to the warnings. Both his Ma, Pa and Rachel's Ma told them about the wrath to come. They warned them of deception sweeping the world. Josh didn't take the need to be born again seriously. He thought there was lots of time to consider Christ's claims to be the way, the truth, and the life. How wrong they were.

Josh's mind drifted back to his dream — pulled straight out of the book of Revelation. He watched a black apocalyptic horse ride across the sky.

"Didn't the four horses stand for God's judgment? The black horse stood for famine. Crops failed for years now. It's a miracle some of my crops grew this year. Now they'll be ruined as no one'll be there to harvest them."

Josh found things made sense when he processed his thoughts aloud.

"World-wide famine is a reality — a bag of oranges costs fifty dollars! Lots of folks barely have enough to eat. Folks are coming from

the cities begging for food — some farmers have been threatened at gunpoint. Folks are desperate."

The chickens listened quietly to Josh's reverie. His Rapture dream was really more like a nightmare. *"No wonder God's judgments are being poured out. Abominations are so prevalent—God's heart must be grieved. How can people be so depraved? Many folks are murdering babies — millions of them — just like when Israel sacrificed to Moloch and Baal. God destroyed civilizations in the past because of this atrocity. It's getting crazy out there."* A verse came to mind...

> *"Because knowing God, they didn't glorify him as God, and didn't give thanks, but became vain in their reasoning, and their senseless heart was darkened. Professing themselves to be wise, they became fools..."*
> Romans 1:21-22

"When people abandon God, He abandons them. Why can't people see that? Men are doing shameful things with men and women with women. People are worshipping and serving things God created instead of the Creator! Why are they so blind? Can't they see what they're doing is wrong? There's no reasoning with some folks!"

He felt such passion about what he was saying Josh couldn't help speaking louder.

"Such insanity! No wonder God abandoned them to their foolish thinking and let them do things that should never be done! He's fed up with their wickedness!"

Josh's voice got even louder as he quoted what he recalled of a verse.

"So many lives are becoming evil! Folks without God are becoming so sinful — greedy — backstabbers — haters of God — proud — boastful. They invent new ways of sinning — breaking their promises — they're heartless — have no mercy! God's justice requires death to all who do such things. Those folks know that — yet they're wicked anyway. Worse, they encourage others to do evil."

Josh didn't hear the men coming into the barn until he heard loud voices in the barn below. Thankfully, they were so noisy they hadn't heard him. He'd have to be careful. The men were discussing what current government taxes would be on the sale of a cow.

"Is it worth taking my cow to market?" Josh recognized Tom's voice.

Another voice piped up, "The government taxes will take ninety percent!"

Tom had been a dairy farmer since he was a boy helping his dad. This was his life. He didn't know how long he could carry on with such huge losses when he sold milk or a cow.

"It's insane — I don't know how a farmer's s'posed to live — the milk quota system is totally in the government's favor," Tom lamented.

A voice Josh didn't recognize spoke up. Was it Earl? The voice sounded like Earl's — but different — this voice spat out bitterness and hatred.

"If you ship too much milk — more than your quota — you has to pay a fine."

Another voice complained, "If we ship too little, we also has to pay a fine. If we sell privately, we is fined."

"Government taxes on feed and the farm are crazy. It's becomin' a losin' proposition," Tom complained.

If he walked away from the farm no one would buy it — well, maybe Earl — but he would have to sell at a great loss.

Josh could tell his friend was desperate. Poor Tom. His dreams were being dashed and broken. He wanted to shout out, "*It'll be okay, buddy!*" — but he made himself stay quiet. People being hunted don't yell out.

Tom relied on Josh, since the disappearance, for guidance and direction. He had always considered Josh a wiser, older brother. Tom wanted to live a godly life — be a man of integrity — but it was getting harder. He could barely make ends meet to support his wife and two sons. He risked being imprisoned by cheating the government out of taxes — but he had to. If he didn't keep back some tax money his family would starve.

The world was so much darker than anyone imagined it would become. Because of the violence and immorality on TV, his friend Josh blasted his TV with his 22. Tom joined him. They didn't want it corrupting the minds and hearts of their families. Tom's wife Sally was not amused.

"Tom, you're taking things way too far."

Sally was addicted to the TV. It mesmerized her. She mindlessly sat from one show to the next — the hypnotic messages were woven into her heart and soul. Tom tried to explain the immorality on TV was poisoning their family and that was unacceptable. Sally didn't agree. Tom tried to make it clearer,

"Sally, those programs you and the boys are watchin' are fillin' your heads with vile things. They're showin' full-blown nudity at a time when our boys are watchin' TV. They have reruns of *Virgin Territory* — where people are trying to lose their virginity. There's a show called *An Affair to Remember* that pushes adultery! I don't want our boys watchin' that garbage."

"Tom, you're takin' this way too far. Those shows ain't all that bad."

"Sally, are you kiddin' me? The commercials are pushin' dating websites for married people to find folks to have affairs with. There's so many murders, rapes and assaults — I don't want our boys fillin' their heads with all that trash. I heard a child will see at least 200,000 acts of violence on TV before they're 18 years old. That's just plain wrong. What's that gonna do to an impressionable mind?"

"Tom, honestly — what's wrong with you?"

"Sally, can't you see? TV's promotin' livin' together before folks get married. They don't even see it's wrong — they've been so brainwashed. Many now believe sex outside of marriage is just fine and dandy. Well — it's not. That's just askin' for trouble."

"Tom, you're so darned old-fashioned."

"Maybe it's cause I just woke up and smelled the coffee. Did you know the States has the highest rate of STDs in the world?

Doesn't that seem strange to you? We ship more porn than any other country. We have huge numbers of abortions. It's the number one cause of death in the U.S. So many homes are broken cause of immorality. It's just wrong, Sally. If the TV's contributin' to that mess, I don't want it in my home."

"It's just entertainment, Tom. No harm in a bit of entertainment."

"Sally, that's what the folks promotin' this garbage want us to think. We're told it's just entertainment — but that's a lie. It's spewing out garbage. Yesterday I saw our boys watchin' a program tellin' them all about witchcraft — how to cast spells and curse folks. They're being told how to contact demons for power. Talking to the dead is encouraged on kids shows. It's changing our kids. It's teaching them to disrespect their parents.

"Tom, I can't believe you're sayin' all this…"

"Satan is trying to capture the hearts of our kids. Don't you see? He's tryin' to capture you, Sally. Those TV programs are destroyin' us. They've been showing reruns of the *Lucifer* show — the one that makes Satan look like a good guy. He's not! He's out to rob, kill, and destroy us, Sally. He despises us. We've gotta put a stop to the brainwashin'. The Bible says in *2 Timothy 3:1-5*

"But know this: that in the last days,
grievous times will come.
For men will be lovers of self, lovers of money,
boastful, arrogant, blasphemers,
disobedient to parents, unthankful, unholy,
without natural affection, unforgiving,
slanderers, without self-control, fierce,
not lovers of good, traitors,
headstrong, conceited, lovers of pleasure
rather than lovers of God,
holding a form of godliness, but having denied its power.
Turn away from these, also."

"That's exactly what TV's promoting, Sally. We need to turn away from the mess."

Sally didn't want to hear it. She said shooting the TV was extreme and joined the children when they complained. She got fed up with Tom's trying to live a life of integrity. She was bored without her TV blaring night and day so she packed up the boys and moved to her mother's.

A few weeks later Tom was served notice by the sheriff — Sally was suing for divorce. She demanded half the value of the farm. She wouldn't allow Tom to see his children — told a lawyer he was mentally and physically abusive — possibly insane. It wasn't true, but the court sided with her.

Tom was heartbroken — devastated. He had no money. He couldn't pay her. This was the only cow he could spare or he couldn't keep up with his milk quota. It was ridiculous. The cow was worth over a thousand dollars. He'd probably end up with a hundred dollars for her — if he was lucky. He owed Sally thousands.

"I don't know what to do. I'm about to lose everything."

One of the voices spoke up, "Tom, did ya' know there's a bounty on Josh's head? I heard he's a criminal." It was definitely Earl's voice.

Another voice piped up, "Yep. I heard that too, Tom. I heard it's a few thousand dollars."

Josh tried not to breathe too loudly.

Rachel

*"Who can find a worthy woman?
For her price is far above rubies."
Proverbs 31:10*

Something flew by Josh's head. Only a bat. As he lay in the hayloft, Josh wondered how he could possibly rescue his girls.

"How do you find people when you don't even know where they are? It's like searching for a needle in a mound of hay." Josh watched the bat darting for bugs.

"Rachel, what a gift from God you are."

Josh never imagined he would meet such an incredible woman while he was deployed to Afghanistan. He first saw her at a coffee shop among the Turkish water pipes and Persian carpets. She looked so calm — so peaceful — he felt drawn to her. Her blonde hair and blue eyes looked so out of place amongst the dark beards and keffiyeh covered heads. He had never seen such a beautiful woman in his life and wondered what she was doing in the middle of a war zone. Josh tried to be as inconspicuous as possible as he slowly moved closer to sit near her table.

He had to hear her voice. It was so gentle — so calming. The New York accent was fascinating.

Picking at his food, he was riveted to Rachel's conversations with those suffering PTSD. She was so kind and compassionate. That must have been a healing balm to those who were in the depths of despair.

"Hey Sam, what do you know about the new psychologist?"

Sam had the scoop on everyone. He was the most loyal friend Josh ever had — trusted him with his life.

"You mean the stunning new doctor?"

"Yeah, that's the one."

"She has a doctorate in clinical psychology. The Marine Corps heard of her success with folks suffering PTSD — so they invited her to Afghanistan."

Josh knew Post Traumatic Stress Disorder was wreaking havoc with the soldiers. There were terrifying events happening on a daily basis in Afghanistan. Soldiers saw scenes of unspeakable horror — flashbacks and nightmares immobilized people — many couldn't carry on. They needed help.

"Sam, people have seen so many horrific things it's a wonder anyone's sane."

"Yeah, I heard alcohol and opioids addictions are huge."

"Some folks are suicidal," Josh added.

"I've heard with Rachel's care many are recovering."

Rachel was honored to be invited by the US Military to serve as a doctor with the Marines and agreed to a two-year posting. She had no idea what she was signing up for. Shortly after arriving at the base in Kandahar, Rachel sent her mom a few letters. After living her entire life in New York City, she could barely put her culture shock of Afghanistan into words.

MANHUNT

Dear Mom,

How are you? I hope all is well. I miss you terribly already. I've arrived safely at the base. The flights were fine but my luggage was lost. Thankfully there was nothing of great importance. Well — I do miss my stash of vitamins and my running shoes.

Afghanistan is not at all what I expected. It's snowing here! Who knew it snows in a desert? I wasn't prepared for the dust, the mud and the poverty. You rarely see women, but when you do, the very traditional women are draped in heavy looking black cloth. They call it a burqa. Less conservative women wear a dress with loose-fitting pants. They wear a chador or head covering. The men wear comfortable looking baggy trousers, tunics and turbans.

I feel conspicuous when I go into town because I look so different from the locals. Thankfully, there's a coffee shop fairly close to the base so I don't have to travel far. It's a bit hard to breathe there because the air is so thick with the smell of strong Turkish tobacco — but the atmosphere is friendly and the coffee is heavenly. When they bake a kind of a baklava pastry the place smells amazing. I've noticed I'm the only woman there — so I'm wondering if it's culturally acceptable for me to be sitting amongst only men. No one seems to mind I'm there so I'll just keep going.

The coffee shop serves meals so it's been fun trying out local foods. I've discovered such delicious dishes it's tempting to go there every night. Kabuli palaw is my new favorite. I think it's their national dish. It's a rice pilaf made with raisins, carrots, lamb and some yummy spices I haven't figured out yet.

You know how much I love East Indian naan bread. I couldn't believe it. It's the most popular bread in Afghanistan! There's a baker close to the base and some days you can smell when he's baking naan.

I hope you visit one day. I miss you. Hug Boots for me.

Love,

Rachel

xo

Dear Mom,

    I went to the market for the first time yesterday. It was cool — you'd love it! There are booths filled with leather purses, gorgeous jewelry, exquisite silks and brocades. The Pushtun women's clothing has such rich colors — Pushtun's are the largest ethnic group in Afghanistan. The women embroider little mirrors all over the front of their garments. It's gorgeous.

    The food stands at the market are enticing. The fruit and vegetables are abundant and exotic. The apricots are fragrant with a rose and peach blush. You know how I love apricots. They are so sweet and delicious here. Muskmelons, pomegranates and mulberries are everywhere. They have staples like sugar, dried beans, barley, wheat, maize, and rice piled on carpets. You buy what you want by the scoop.

    I had to walk through a herd of Marco Polo sheep with their massive curved horns to get to the coffee shop today. Streets are often filled with camels, cows, horses, and goats. I guess it's the fastest route for a shepherd to get his animals from one pasture to another. Animals are as common on the streets as people. You have to be careful where you walk — just imagine the smells.

    There are colorful parrots squawking in the trees outside my tent right now. A red-rumped swallow is trying to make a nest in the corner of my tent. I hope she's successful. Every morning I wake up to the cooing of rock doves. It's such a soothing sound.

    The sights, sounds, and smells of Afghanistan are almost indescribable. It's quite the adventure being here. I really hope you can visit. I miss you so much. Hugs to you and Boots.

                                                Love.
                                                Rachel
                                                xo

MANHUNT

Dear Mom,

    This is not what I signed up for. My medical training didn't prepare me for this. Normal techniques don't work here — the trauma is too deep. Honestly, it's crazy here mom. My first few weeks I wasn't convinced I could make a difference so I was ready to pack up and go home. But you know me — I'm not a quitter. I came here to make a difference so I'm determined to do that.

    I wondered how I could possibly develop relationships with my patients in a caring environment in the middle of a war zone. So — I decided to meet my patients in the coffee shop I told you about. I thought it would be non-threatening to meet as friends and would provide the best kind of therapy. I decided to give it a try. Nothing ventured nothing gained, right? I call these meetings therapeutic alliances.

    I mostly just listen. It seems to be working as the commanding officer said he is noticing lives are being changed. That's pretty incredible when you realize many of these people have developed horrendous addictions to cope with their trauma. This is harder than anything I've ever experienced. Life is pretty raw here.

    On a different note, I'm sure you'll find this interesting. There is a tall, dark-haired, handsome Marine who shows up often at the coffee shop during my therapeutic alliances. I'm not sure if this is coincidental or if he's stalking me. He always sits at the table beside me and looks like he's not interested in the conversations — but he seems to be listening to every word. Either that or he just really loves lots of strong coffee. It's kind of intriguing. If this isn't coincidental, he must have pulled a lot of strings to be available during my crazy schedule. I heard him ordering a coffee. He has the deepest Southern drawl I've ever heard. His voice is gorgeous.

> Hug Boots for me.
> I miss you and my fat cat.
> Love,
> Rachel
> Xo

"Do you think Rachel thinks I'm stalking her?" Josh asked.

Sam squinted his green eyes, rubbed his short-cropped hair, and asked, "Why?"

"Well — I found her work schedule. It listed her daily meetings. I wonder if she's noticed I'm sitting at the table next to her often."

"Don't scare the girl, Josh. Maybe don't show up at *every* meeting. That *is* stalking…"

"It's her eyes, Sam. Her eyes kinda mesmerize me. Her voice — it's so soothing. I love her New York accent. She's irresistible. Abdul-Karim must love me. I have never drunk so much coffee in all my life."

"Sounds like you are smitten," Sam laughed.

Josh was shocked as he realized it was probably true. He loved Rachel and he hadn't even spoken a word to her. How was that possible?

"I should fake PTSD. She'd have to talk to me."

"That's crazy, Josh. Just ask her for a date."

"Oh — I hadn't thought of that. What a great idea. But where would I take her? It's dangerous to go off the base at night."

"Josh, my boy. You're creative. Give it some thought."

Rachel said yes! Would Friday night ever arrive? Why did he make it four days away? Did this amazing woman really accept a date with him? Could there be any greater joy on earth? The butterflies in his stomach were having a party.

Sam helped set up their tent like an inviting café — well, as much as they could in an army base in Afghanistan. Josh went to the open-air market and bargained for everything from pillows to pastries. Sam volunteered to be the waiter.

Friday night took years to arrive. Josh was so excited he thought his heart would burst.

Rachel looked stunning — Josh couldn't take his eyes off her — so he didn't notice the chair he fell over. He felt like a silly, love-struck teenager. Rachel pretended not to notice. Sam sat in the corner laughing so hard Josh glared at him. Ignoring the glare, Sam nonchalantly picked up an instrument to play some background music. He was the maître-de, waiter, and entertainer.

"Josh, where did you ever find such exotic silks?"

"I raided the market. Abdul said I'm on his favorite customer list."

Rachel laughed.

"Josh, the tent looks awesome. The candlelight — the music — it's all so beautiful. Thank you."

"You're welcome, Ma'am. I enjoyed putting this together."

"What's that instrument?"

"It's called an 'oud'. It's a short-necked fretless lute. It's common in Arabic music. I think Sam plays it fairly well."

"I just picked it up recently. Sorry I don't play professionally," Sam laughed.

"I love it, Sam. It sounds a bit like a classical guitar."

"I'm glad you like it."

Rachel was so lost in the music it took a moment for Josh to recapture her attention.

"Rachel…"

Rachel snapped out of her reverie and smiled at Josh.

"Because of fire hazards in the tents, I had to ask permission to use candles. When I told them it was for you, permission was granted. Everyone loves you." Under his breath Josh added, *"Especially me"*.

The waiter brought a large tray of food to the table.

"Wow, Josh. What a feast — lamb, falafel, hummus, salad, pastries, Turkish coffee. All for us? How did you ever get all this?"

"Connections my dear. Connections."

Sam continued the oud serenade as they enjoyed the meal.

"Josh, could you please ask the waiter to bring more coffee? It's wonderful."

"Garçon. The lady would like more coffee."

"My pleasure, Mademoiselle."

———

Josh decided his date with Rachel was the most memorable night he ever lived. He couldn't wait to see her again. Tomorrow couldn't come soon enough. They met almost every day for a couple months — mostly just walks around the compound. Anti-aircraft missiles and armored personnel carriers were their seats under the starry skies as they talked. Rachel was the most intriguing woman he had ever met.

"I grew up in Brooklyn, New York, in the Bushwick area." Rachel's face looked sad as she reflected, "It's one of the most dangerous places in New York City. When I was a little girl the buildings were so covered in graffiti you could barely see the bricks."

"Haven't some of the world's best street artists painted wall murals there?" Josh asked.

"How did you know that?"

"I read it somewhere. I like art."

"There's lots of street art now — but back then, growing up, burned out tenement buildings were common. It seemed like a new bar or coffee shop opened every week and closed the following week. I worked at a local bistro to pay my college expenses. Thankfully, that one stayed open."

"You paid for college? I assumed your rich daddy put you through school."

"Nope. Just the opposite. I was one of those poor students who had to work hard to get good grades — I needed scholarships. I chose Pace University in New York because it was close to home so I could live with my mother. If I was away, she would have been alone. Dad checked out when I was five. I heard he was still in New York City — but I never heard from him."

"I'm sorry. It must have been hard having no dad around."

"It was hard — but my mom did her best to give me a good childhood."

"Why did you choose psychology?"

"Crime was crazy in Bushwick when I was a teen. One day, my friend forgot to watch where she was walking. She looked down to read a message on her phone, was grabbed from behind and forced into an abandoned building."

Rachel's eyes filled with tears.

"The resulting guilt and shame nearly destroyed her. Carol suffered severe depression and PTSD from when she was sixteen to twenty. I watched my friend spiral into a dark pit and there seemed to be no way to reach her. She attempted suicide. Her parents were desperate.

They finally found a clinical psychologist who took my friend out for coffee and let her talk. That's where I got my idea for my therapeutic alliances. After each meeting we could see the darkness slowly leaving. We were so relieved and thankful to see the hopelessness replaced with hope. That's when I knew what I wanted to do with my life."

"Rachel, that's sad about your friend — but it led you to be who you are. People can't help but notice the caring way you treat others."

"I love working with my patients. It's fulfilling seeing them developing ways of coping in spite of being traumatized and depressed."

"Well, I've heard these meetings have made all the difference for many people. You've made great progress in a matter of months."

"Thank you. It's rewarding to see people find hope and a reason to live again."

"You are helping folks get their lives back."

"Thank you, Josh. Why did you join the military?"

"Well, I grew up on a farm in Alabama with very patriotic parents. They love the U.S. and the freedoms we've always enjoyed there. They thank God often they live in a prosperous nation founded on Biblical principles. Because of my patriotic roots, I felt compelled to join the Marines to protect the freedom of our nation."

"I'm grateful for the men and women who joined the peace keeping forces to keep America free, Josh."

"I was told from childhood I must stand up for my country and defend other nation's freedoms. Pa always quoted *Psalm 33:12*, *"Blessed is the nation whose God is the LORD."*"

"You're a good man, Josh. I sensed that a while ago. I respect and admire you for the man you are. It takes great courage to be here to protect the people of Afghanistan. You're putting your life on the line being here."

"That's mighty kind of you, Ma'am. I'm proud to be an American and a Marine."

"Josh, I love your Southern drawl."

"Why thank you again, Ma'am. I love your 'Yankee' accent."

Josh soon realized Rachel was as beautiful inside as she was outside. He knew he would never find another woman like her. What if she was deployed elsewhere? What if he never saw her again? That was a disheartening thought. Maybe it was because he had no idea how long they would live — life was fragile in Afghanistan — Josh came up with a brilliant idea.

"Rachel, I realize we've only dated a few months…" Josh hesitated.

"…but I've stalked you for several months before that so I feel like I've known you for years."

"So — it wasn't coincidental you were at the coffee shop nearly every time I was," Rachel laughed.

"Nope. It sure wasn't a coincidence. I had to pull a lot of strings to make that happen. Ever since I saw you, I was drawn to you, Rachel."

"That's sweet, Josh. I was attracted to you too. Don't think for a second I didn't notice this handsome man sitting next to me. I looked forward to seeing you and was disappointed the few times you weren't there. I was hoping you'd finally get the courage to ask me out. I even wrote my mom about you."

"You did? What did you say to her?"

Rachel laughed. "That's classified information, Josh."

After a short silence, Josh said quietly, "I love you, Rachel."

Josh paused to see how Rachel would react. She didn't seem alarmed by his confession so he decided it was safe to continue.

"I love you with all my heart."

He hoped this didn't sound like complete lunacy and was overjoyed to hear Rachel say,

"I love you too, Josh."

Josh's heart beat faster as he continued.

"I have enjoyed every moment with you, Rachel. I am so in love with you. I can't imagine my life without you in it."

"I can't imagine my life without you either, Josh. You're a very special man."

"I have something very important to ask you."

Josh paused. Was the top of an armored personnel carrier really the place he wanted to propose to this beautiful woman?

He looked at her smile — her sparkling blue eyes — and decided he couldn't wait. He hoped this would be a romantic memory for Rachel.

"Rachel, my love. Will you marry me?"

Josh held his breath — waiting for a reply.

"I'll have to think about that."

"Are you done thinking yet?"

"Yes, Josh. I'd love to marry you, my darling man."

Josh was positive his heart was going to burst it was so full of love and joy.

Dear Mom,

    I don't know if you're going to believe this! You know the handsome Marine I wrote you about? The one I thought was stalking me in the coffee shop? I was right. He was! Lucky me!

    He is honestly the sweetest, kindest, most thoughtful, funny, hands-down most romantic man I've ever met. His name is Joshua Williams. We've only been dating a few months — but I love him. Mom, I realize this might sound crazy. He asked me to marry him and I said yes!!! I hope this doesn't sound like complete insanity. I understand you might be a bit skeptical because of how things went for you and dad. I'm sorry it didn't work out better for you. I know you warned me to be careful — to guard my heart — but this man is not dad. I'm sure he would never hurt me.

    Are you available to come to Afghanistan for our wedding in a couple months? We set the date for July 21st. Josh wanted to get married as soon as possible, but I want to give you enough notice so you can request time off from your work at the art museum, arrange your flights, and find a home for Boots for a few weeks. If you can come, I would love to have you as my matron of honor. It would be special for me to have you here. You are my only family.

    I have so much to tell you — like all about our incredible first date. Josh must have spent his entire pay for a month on a traditional Afghan dinner and making his tent look exotic for me. I can't wait to tell you the details. I hope you can come. Let me know what you decide as soon as possible. Hug Boots for me. I miss you.

                                            Much love,
                                            Rachel
                                            xo

Friends picked baskets full of fragrant red roses and deep scarlet poppies from nearby fields to adorn the mess tent. It soon resembled a lovely garden. They had to use the biggest tent because the entire base was invited.

Joy and rejoicing floated among the guests — the happiness felt so real you could almost touch it. Becky, Rachel's mom, was the lovely matron of honor.

"Honey, you look so beautiful," Josh whispered as they stood in front of the chaplain. Josh could hardly contain his happiness. He wondered how he deserved such joy.

"You look gorgeous — so handsome," Rachel whispered from under her lace veil. Her silk dress moved gently in the breeze. The rose garland on her head and the roses in the room wafted a heady, sweet perfume through the air. Rachel felt like a beautiful princess in a romantic fairytale.

Smiling at Josh through tears of joy — Rachel was sure she was the luckiest woman who ever lived. Could life get any better?

Josh lay in the barn loft thinking about the beauty, the hopes, dreams and promises of that day. How quickly our dreams can be dashed.

We had no idea an enormous storm cloud hung over our lives — ready to crash around us. Rachel, I never meant to hurt or disappoint you. I'm so sorry, my love.

News

*"In the latter time of their kingdom, when
the transgressors have come to the full,
a king of fierce face, and understanding
dark sentences, will stand up.
His power will be mighty, but not by his own power.
He will destroy awesomely, and will
prosper in what he does.
He will destroy the mighty ones and the holy people."
Daniel 8:23-24*

MANHUNT

The droning of flies and cackling of chickens made sleep impossible. Josh considered how the world changed — descended into chaos — since the disappearance. So much happened in such a short time — it was crazy. Millions vanished. It was seemingly impossible but true.

Josh stiffened when he heard the barn door latch being lifted. Someone came creaking up the stairs to the loft. Sinking deeper into the hay, Josh heard Tom muttering.

"Fifty dollars from the sale of that darn stupid cow! That's all I got — fifty dollars!!! How's a man s'posed to live on fifty dollars?"

Josh almost spoke up. He wanted to say something — anything — to comfort his friend. He also wanted to ask Tom for food and medicine for his torn leg — but speaking didn't seem wise. Josh held his peace while Tom threw a few bales down to the barn floor for his hungry cows. Josh lay still as Tom's feet came dangerously close to his head.

Finally, creaking could be heard as Tom descended the ladder. Josh never dreamed he'd live to see the day he'd be relieved to see his friend leave.

His heart pounded long after Tom left the barn. His thoughts about the crazy times people found themselves in continued. It was unbelievable when millions vanished in a millisecond — everywhere — throughout the entire world. Some said the disappearance was the Rapture spoken about in the Bible. Others had different thoughts about space alien abductions — not many agreed. Josh recalled the reports that tried to explain the disappearances.

There were those who quoted the ancient Book — said it had been foretold Jesus would come for those who watched for Him — who understood this world was not their home. Although no one actually saw it happen — many suspected the Lord took folks to meet Him in the air. Jesus warned He would come as a thief in the night. He advised people to be ready.

Many who professed to be believers hadn't taken the warnings to heart. They had been caught up with the affairs of this life — Jesus was not their first love. They were shocked to have been left behind.

From what he later read in the Bible, Josh realized the days to come would be savage. He marveled again how the world descended into chaos in moments.

Ships collided in the oceans.

Planes crashed to the ground as pilots vanished.

Airports shut down — flights were grounded — flight crews disappeared.

Trains derailed.

Doctors — in the midst of performing surgeries — disappeared.

Power plants ground to a halt — hydroelectric dams couldn't function without engineers.

Stores, banks and schools closed.

Anarchy ensued.

Riots broke out.

Thieves rampaged.

Buildings were looted.

Fires exploded in the streets.

There were massive car pile-ups as driverless vehicles plowed into oncoming traffic.

Underground subways halted — passengers ran screaming down the tracks into the darkness.

Pandemonium and utter confusion ensued.

The news media trumpeted the announcements—

SPACE ALIENS ABDUCT MILLIONS!!!
ALIENS REMOVE ALL REBELS!!!
PEOPLE BEAMED ONTO ALIEN SPACEHIPS!!!

Photos of aliens descending in their space crafts appeared on newspaper covers. 'Aliens' were interviewed on television. They said they were ambassadors from far off galaxies and had come to help with earth's evolution. They said they had been assigned to be keepers and overlords of humanity and were sent to serve mankind.

The aliens were small, emaciated, and gray — they looked like grotesquely disfigured humans with totally black eyes and raspy, wheezing voices. Anyone who stood near them said the stench was overpowering — like sulphur or rotten eggs. They had a vile, evil look — but most people bought the story. After all, why would these creatures lie to them? They assured the masses they could be trusted.

People were informed the ones who disappeared were rebels — were being transported to another planet to continue their evolution. They explained the missing ones weren't ready for the glorious 'New World Order' that was about to appear on earth. Only the enlightened and evolved were left. It would be a spectacular new day for the world. Many thought this made sense. They rejoiced because they were considered the "enlightened ones".

Shortly after the disappearance, the aliens announced a great king was willing to step up — embrace the chaos — and rescue them. They reported he would soon appear.

The people of earth waited expectantly.

One day, "the king" arrived out of nowhere — displaying spectacular signs — causing fire to come down from Heaven.

> *"...even he whose coming is according*
> *to the working of Satan*
> *with all power and signs and lying wonders..."*
> *2 Thessalonians 2: 9*

The media proclaimed —

MESSIAH HAS COME!!!
PEACE AND SAFETY IN OUR TIMES!!!

People rejoiced.

They reverently stood in awe as he was introduced on the world stage. Massive celebrations erupted throughout the world. A hologram image of the king appeared at every celebration so he seemed to be present everywhere. People fell to their knees weeping with joy — adoringly worshipping him.

The king made a great speech — instantly translated into every earth language. The world declared, "It is the voice of a god and not of a man!"

He announced he was the Christ — but would allow the people of earth to call him *Messiah, Mahdi, Lord Most High, Lord Maitreya,* or *King.*

*"For many will come in my name,
saying, 'I am the Christ,'
and will lead many astray.
Matthew 24:5*

The king spoke hypnotically. Crowds were mesmerized — just like Eve had once been in an ancient garden.

Who was he? Some said he was the "light bringer" — the epitome of knowledge — a dispeller of ignorance and illusion. Some said he was the embodiment of complete bliss — a bestower of wisdom — the destroyer of fear of birth and death.

Where did he come from? Some said he came from the Himalayas.

No one knew for sure.

No one cared.

People welcomed him.

Because of satellite communication the king's actions could be followed live. People were enamored as they watched fierce, dark clouds whirling over his head and lightning bolts flashing above him as he spoke.

This raw power was exciting.

This was the man they had been waiting for.

The masses pledged allegiance to this king.

Josh was surprised the world was so desperate to welcome this unknown man. It didn't seem to matter to anyone when it was announced he was transhuman. Josh wondered if he was like the Nephilim of old — part fallen angel and part man — genetically altered — a superhuman. Was his mind so enhanced that his thought processes were far beyond a human's ability to think?

MANHUNT

People didn't care if he was a man or a demon as long as he brought peace and safety to earth.

The man who called himself king told the people of earth they were as sheep without a shepherd. He would willingly be their good shepherd. He promised his light, love and power would restore the plan on earth. He didn't elaborate what that plan was. Josh was sure it was one that began with a serpent in a garden.

Ambitious and transformational ideas to eradicate poverty and world hunger were proclaimed. It all sounded wonderful — too good to be true. He told people there would be lasting protection of earth and its resources.

Discrimination would be a thing of the past. It would be a tolerant, just, socially inclusive world. Inequalities and borders between countries would be abolished. Global peace and safety would be guaranteed — however, he forgot to mention that would be for an elite few.

He wooed the masses with appealing promises — soothing, mesmerizing words. They didn't see the trap wrapped in a charming package.

> *"For when they are saying, "Peace and safety,"*
> *then sudden destruction will come on them,*
> *like birth pains on a pregnant woman.*
> *Then they will in no way escape."*
> 1 Thessalonians 5:3

The aliens — demons — were beside themselves with excitement at the arrival of the king.

They told news reporters it would now be a golden era for earth.

There would be world peace — now that the unenlightened ones who held up earth's evolution were gone.

Chaos would end.

Justice would prevail.

His first announcement as king, infused the people with hope.

A seven-year Peace Treaty with Israel was to be signed. This was of global importance. The Jews were elated — world terrorism would finally be over.

The ancient scrolls were being fulfilled — the promised Messiah had finally come. This was the answer to thousands of years of prayers.

Messiah would allow the temple to be rebuilt and would allow the high priest to resume the ancient sacrificial system. The priests were ready. They had been carefully screened to be sure they had Cohen DNA. These were direct descendants of Aaron, the first High priest.

They had prepared for this day. The priestly garments hung in readiness. The blood of innocent animals would again be shed for the sins of the Jewish nation. Red heifers had been carefully selected and bred to be sacrificed. Jacob's mottled, multi-horned sheep were flown from Canada and corralled — waiting their place on the altar. All the implements to be used in the temple were fashioned. The solid gold menorah stood sentinel over the Western Wall, waiting its placement in the third temple.

Everything was in readiness.

The earth seemed to hold its breath in anticipation.

Then — as if someone released a high-pressure valve — there was an explosion of jubilant dancing in the streets of Israel.

God heard their cries! The Peace Treaty was signed!

The king promised his loyal subjects there would be global peace — no more wars. But there were. Wars and rumors of wars increased. Nations rose against nations, and kingdoms against kingdoms. The king sent Artificial Intelligence troops to quell all uprisings — but lawlessness abounded. Many false prophets rose up — deceiving many — saying the king would alleviate all suffering on earth — but he didn't.

The king promised to end poverty — there would be health and well-being for all. Instead, there was great suffering — life became unbearable. People longed for death but it eluded them.

MANHUNT

The king announced global hunger would stop — yet people were starving in the streets. It was worse than anything anyone had ever seen.

The next announcement caused some to pause in their celebrations.

Wait — what did he just say?

The king decreed earth could not maintain its present population. There would be a culling. The king hadn't mentioned before his great ideas involved most of the planet's population being decimated.

A law was passed — anyone over fifty years old must report for euthanasia unless they had special government decreed immunity. The people wholeheartedly agreed with the king's plan. Fifty seemed like a fair age. People were told they would be reincarnated so it wasn't really death — more like a rebirth of sorts. The king was gracious — giving people the chance to be born again. There were special euthanasia hospices where people were shown movies of breathtakingly beautiful earth scenes while they were quietly drugged to death. It was all so peaceful. So tidy. The law was soon expanded to include anyone with a disfigurement or a disability.

A few questioned this law. They disappeared.

"There's no need for alarm," the king said as he smiled charmingly into the camera. "When there are less people there will be peace and plenty for all."

People trusted their Messiah. They comforted themselves by saying his plans were for their good. He knew what was best.

The king's next decree, after the Peace Treaty with Israel and enforced euthanasia, was the division of the earth into ten quadrants. He based the divisions on the Club of Rome guidelines created in 1973. This new global order would divide the world into ten economic trading blocks. The king didn't mention there would be regional control, based upon a ruling class living in luxury, operating within a technocracy. It would be a total surveillance state controlled by an elite government and technical experts.

In this new system all of society would be managed by a cashless technology. This global monetary system was to be implemented to ensure the ending of looting and crime, however, criminals will always find ways to carry out their schemes.

Artificial Intelligence would control the masses. Facial recognition cameras and drones would be everywhere and could recognize a person in nanoseconds. This would be a far more effective method of controlling the masses than any previous political system. The world would be interconnected as never before.

The king would have absolute power and authority in every area of life. The movements of every person would be tracked and monitored. This system assigned privileges for good behavior and cut off access to life sustaining aid for any infractions. Of course, the king hadn't told the adoring masses they would be controlled. The crowds worshipped him. He planned to keep it that way.

Algorithms would scan all phone calls and emails for any unapproved speech. Punishments for infractions would be swift and fierce. Such power never existed before.

Folks applauded when the king decreed sex with anyone of any age was approved. Babies and children were now considered fair game—child molestation would be legal. Pedophiles rejoiced. The king didn't recognize Jesus had made a binding decree thousands of years previously,

> *"Whoever receives one such little child*
> *in my name receives me,*
> *but whoever causes one of these little ones*
> *who believe in me to stumble,*
> *it would be better for him if a huge*
> *millstone were hung around his neck*
> *and that he were sunk in the depths of the sea."*
> *Matthew 18:5-6*

MANHUNT

A large portion of land was set aside in each of earth's ten quadrants as a home for the beasts. The large tracts of land had to be fenced or no one would have survived. No one could pass through the Territories. It was too dangerous. Half of the old United States was a sanctuary for the beasts.

These were not ordinary beasts. They were evil — genetically engineered. Behemoth stood in the rivers with bones like tubes of bronze and limbs like bars of iron. There were lion-eagle hybrid creatures, and huge bull-like creatures with a single unicorn horn for goring. Bears with massive iron teeth and claws, and a leopard-like creature with four wings and four heads, roamed the Territories. A beast with ten horns and teeth of iron emerged from the sea. One creature who looked like a dragon — spoke like a lamb — rose out of the earth. These last two kept the rest of the beast population from exceeding the capacity of the land. Anyone displeasing the king was banished to the Territories or guillotined.

> *"I will send on you famine and evil*
> *animals, and they will bereave you.*
> *Pestilence and blood will pass through you.*
> *I will bring the sword on you. I, Yahweh, have spoken it."*
> Ezekiel 5:17

The king used this last exceedingly terrible beast to represent his kingdom. The dragon image appeared on the king's flags, banners and Great Seal.

All media announced if anyone foolishly believed *Jesus Christ* was the *Messiah*, the *Son of God*, the true *King of kings* and *Lord of lords*, they would be delivered to the Grand Tribunal. This was made up of the Administrators of the One World Religion — the False Prophet, the Antichrist, and the Beast.

The Bible said the number of the Beast is 666 — the number of the Emperor of the revived Roman Empire. That number was embedded into the king's nanotechnology programs.

Anyone knowing the whereabouts of professing Christians would be rewarded for turning them in to the Grand Tribunal. The king wanted no allegiances to any power or authority but him. Some recognized what was happening — they had missed the Rapture and knew they would face the wrath of God and the terror of the king. Many who became Christ followers after the Rapture, tried to escape by abandoning their homes, lands, and everything they owned. They couldn't find a welcoming place — friends and family closed doors in their faces. They were told to leave and never come back. These desperate people wandered without homes — dwelling in deserts, mountains, dens and caves of the earth. They were told if they would only worship the king all would be well.

> *"Then they will deliver you up to*
> *oppression and will kill you.*
> *You will be hated by all of the nations*
> *for My name's sake."*
> Matthew 24:9

It was decreed anyone professing Christ to be the true and rightful King would be beheaded.

Many betrayed family and friends to save their own lives. Anyone suspected of having unofficial political beliefs, or religious views other than those officially sanctioned by the king and his prophet, would be imprisoned and killed.

Heat sensing tracking devices were used to locate those who rebelled against the king. Drones were flown to their hiding places with a message from the king — safety and asylum would be granted to any who returned home. Several who trusted the message discovered their homes were overtaken — they had nowhere to go.

That's when the trucks arrived. Christians were told they would be taken to better facilities. They didn't realize the trucks were headed to the guillotines.

MANHUNT

*"I saw thrones, and they sat on them,
and judgment was given to them.
I saw the souls of those who had been
beheaded for the testimony of Jesus,
and for the word of God, and such as didn't
worship the beast nor his image,
and didn't receive the mark on their
forehead and on their hand.
They lived and reigned with Christ for a thousand years."*
Revelation 20:4

Those who gave up their belief in God and testified the king was god were provided for. They lived in relative security. They sold their eternal souls for some morsels of bread. They forgot that this life is a vapor — they didn't recall the ancient Book says,

*"For what does it profit a man, to gain the
whole world, and forfeit his life?"*
Mark 8:36

PART 2

WHERE WERE YOU, GOD?

Where Were You, God?

*"If I ascend up into Heaven, you are there.
If I make my bed in Sheol, behold, you are there!"
Psalm 139:8*

MANHUNT

There was nothing to do in the hayloft but think — but these particular thoughts were dangerous. They had already stolen so much from Josh's life. This was the first time in years he allowed his thoughts to travel down that dusty road again. He wondered aloud, *"Where were You, God?"*, as he allowed his mind to look at that day from different angles — to see if it made any more sense now.

Their assignment in Afghanistan that day was to hold back any advance of the Taliban. The men in his unit were closer than blood—they were family. They called themselves the Brotherhood — managed for months to hold back the enemy to protect innocent civilians. But not that day.

Josh watched as the scene unfolded again — saw the convoy driving deep into the Hindu Kush Mountains over what was supposed to be an old, abandoned road. It wound through a deep gully they'd been told hadn't seen action for months. Rounding the hill — they saw it — a display presumably set up as a warning to those who dared stray from Allah.

The road was lined with over a dozen crosses. Women hung on them. Hearts had been cut out. Their deaths had been recent. If only they'd arrived sooner. There was a sign nailed on the crosses scrawled in Arabic and Dari. Abdul, a trusted local, translated the words.

Warning!
This is what happens to infidel swine.
This woman loved another God.
His Name is Jesus.

This was more gruesome than anything any of the Marines had ever seen.

That's when the Taliban attacked.

We were trapped—ambushed. Helicopters swooped in just when it looked like we were all dead. It was a miracle they found us.

The Taliban melted into the surrounding mountains as quickly as they appeared.

We lost most of our squadron that day. Only Sam and I survived. I don't know how or why I lived. I wished I had died.

Sam had been hit in the leg. Josh watched in shock as medics loaded his best friend into a chopper. He heard later Sam was transferred to Germany and eventually back to his duty station in Hawaii. Poor Sam — spent a year and a half in surgeries and casts.

Josh stopped his musings long enough to look through a crack in the barn's panels. The guards were still patrolling around his house. The situation looked desperate. "*God,*" he whispered, "*help me know what to do. Should I ask Tom for help?*"

Josh allowed his thoughts to drift back again to Afghanistan.

The emotions were deep — intense. It was crazy — after that day — I tried but I couldn't snap out of the depression. How could anyone understand? They weren't there. I hadn't expected the roller coaster ride my emotions were on. It would seem like I was getting better and then I would have a trigger. Something would remind me of my brothers — a song on the radio — a piece of lemon pie reminding me of Joe's love for it — a woman with long, dark hair.

The grief didn't come in any special order or timeframe — just randomly struck in waves and beat against his soul.

I felt like a lost man stumbling across a desert without a compass or water. Sometimes it felt like my heart was going to break — the pain was so intense I wondered if I was having a heart attack.

Josh sat bolt upright — startled by a sudden noise. It was only a rooster crowing. He muttered, "*Silly bird. It's way past dawn. Shut up!*"

He went back to his thoughts about the day that changed everything. Rachel tried to comfort him but he shut her out — wanted nothing to do with her. He wondered why she kept asking him such stupid questions. He felt like he was being interrogated.

"Josh, talk to me."

"How do you feel?"

"Are you okay?"

"Josh, are you going to eat something?"

"Josh, how are you holding up?"

MANHUNT

Why did she ask such stupid questions? I watched most of my squad blown to smithereens and she wanted to know how I was holding up? I wasn't. Life wasn't the same — never would be — I was not okay — I saw too much. The smell of death was burned into my soul. I couldn't shake the pictures of the women on the crosses and my brothers dying around me.

"I care about you. I love you. Are you listening?"

I was sort-of listening — but it was difficult to hear my wife's words over the sound of the firefight still ringing in my ears. Listening isn't as easy as it appears. Thoughts seem to get in the way. I assumed because I was looking at her — trying to pay attention — I heard her. I realized I hadn't. She was speaking from her heart to my heart. The problem was my heart was cold and there was a wall words couldn't breach.

The old questions that had no answers resurfaced to haunt Josh again.

Why were we in Afghanistan? Did anyone really know? This war — Operation Enduring Freedom — was meant to be a war to stop terrorism. It sounded simple — but it was anything but simple. Sometimes I had the feeling we were there as a military presence to protect resources. Did anyone really care about the people?

Josh replayed the scene several times in his mind — could they have done anything different? His best conclusion was they all should have stayed in bed that day.

I felt a paralyzing sense of loss — life was overwhelming. The despair eventually led to thoughts of suicide. I was positive Rachel would be happier without me. There was nothing to live for. I wanted life to end — the pain was unbearable. How Rachel survived and didn't give up on me is a miracle. The helplessness, hopelessness, and worthlessness I felt incapacitated me. In spite of myself — I had no idea at that time where this desire came from — I decided to live.

Josh recalled the day he and Rachel dropped onto satin pillows in the coffee shop and waited for Mohammed to bring coffees and baklavas. The memory was so vivid it could have been yesterday. This was the place they had first seen each other. It had good memories — safe memories.

"Rachel, thanks for meeting me. This is hard..." Josh fought to find the right words. "I have felt such a sense of loss. My brothers..."

Rachel reached across the table to hold his hand. For the first time in a year Josh didn't pull away. Holding her hand somehow connected him to the real world.

"I can't believe my brothers are gone, Rachel. I felt like I had nothing to live for."

Josh slowly swirled the sugar in his coffee — buying time — not knowing what to say. He glanced at Rachel. What could he possibly say to help heal the brokenness of their shattered lives? He could see the questions in her eyes, *"Can he be trusted — is he going to spiral into darkness and leave me behind again?"*

Time seemed to stand still. They could hear the sheep bleating in the market outside the door and the clinking of glasses as people stirred their coffees. They could smell baklava baking. Men in the market could be heard calling out to customers in Dari, the official Afghan-Persian language.

A light rain was pattering on the clay roof tiles.

Chickens squawked as people shooed them out of the way in the streets.

There was a haunting call to prayer from a dozen minarets.

Josh pulled his thoughts back — this conversation was very important. Having built up the courage to talk to Rachel, he wasn't about to let anything distract him.

"Rachel, I felt darkness in my soul this past year — since that assignment in Kandahar. I wanted life to end. I was positive you'd be better off without me."

He took a few gulps of coffee.

"How you survived and didn't give up on me is a miracle."

A parrot squawked and made Josh jump. He automatically looked around the coffee shop for the gunman.

"It's okay, Josh. You're safe here," Rachel said.

MANHUNT

"Rachel, I read about some courageous people. I want to be like them — but I don't know how."

Rachel was surprised to see Josh pull a tiny Bible from his khaki shirt pocket.

"Where'd you get that?"

"Someone left this old Bible on my bunk — opened to this underlined part in Hebrews."

"Were they trying to tell you something?"

"Maybe. I haven't endured nearly as much as these people."

"Oh?"

"Listen to this, Rachel."

> "...who through faith subdued kingdoms,
> worked out righteousness,
> obtained promises, stopped the mouths of
> lions, quenched the power of fire,
> escaped the edge of the sword, from
> weakness were made strong,
> grew mighty in war, and caused foreign armies to flee.
> Women received their dead by
> resurrection. Others were tortured,
> not accepting their deliverance, that they
> might obtain a better resurrection.
> Others were tried by mocking and scourging,
> yes, moreover by bonds and imprisonment.
> They were stoned. They were sawn
> apart. They were tempted.
> They were slain with the sword. They went
> around in sheep skins and in goat skins;
> being destitute, afflicted, ill-treated —of
> whom the world was not worthy —
> wandering in deserts, mountains, caves,
> and the holes of the earth."
> Hebrews 11:33-38.

"Those people were so strong — I feel so weak."

"They do sound very brave."
"What's wrong with me, Rachel?"

Josh didn't realize how loudly he spoke until the men stopped inhaling on their shish-a pipes to stare at him. He smiled at them until they calmly went back to their pipes.

"I want peace of mind. I want us to have a chance."

They were both crying.

"Rachel, I'm sorry I hurt you."

Her eyes said *I forgive you* and *I love you*. Fumbling in her purse Rachel pulled out a small Bible.

"Where'd that come from?"

"Someone's dropping Bibles all over the base. I found it in the mess tent. Listen to this. A king named David wrote it."

> *"My soul is laid low in the dust.*
> *Revive me according to your word!*
> *My soul is weary with sorrow:*
> *strengthen me according to your word."*
> *Psalm 119: 25, 28*

"Exactly how I feel. I want out of this pit."
"Josh, maybe we need God?"
"Nah, we don't need God. I think man is the only true moral force in the world."

Had I really said we didn't need God? From my vantage point in the barn — years later — I realize what a fool I was. I heard someone say, "We all make choices but ultimately our choices make us." I didn't realize my choice to ignore God and keep Him at arms-length would make our next descent into darkness an even deeper one.

The Pit

"There is no pit so deep, that God's love is not deeper still."
Corrie Ten Boom

MANHUNT

Josh lay in the barn — reminiscing about how life had seemed good again. He recalled his thoughts, *Is it possible? Is the horror of PTSD really over? Am I finally free of the nightmares?* Things seemed normal for the first time in over a year. Colors were vibrant — flowers smelled fragrant — food didn't taste like cardboard. The sun shone brighter — the pain was gone! Freedom never felt so wonderful.

Then — one day — a woman with long, dark hair walked by — a powerful trigger. Horrific scenes flashed to life — larger and more vivid than any previous flashbacks.

Josh's world suddenly went dark. Memories pulled him back to a dusty road — to a grueling march to the backside of the Kandahar Mountains — to a routine reconnaissance mission. As they trudged along the road everything seemed so routine. Then — in a blinding flash — as they rounded a corner — everything changed. He saw the women on the crosses again — faces contorted in agony. His mind moved to the men in the unit who were too young to die — some barely out of their teens. They lay in their own blood. He heard again the guns blazing and the sound of choppers. He watched the Taliban — like wisps of brown and black cloth — disappear into the surrounding mountains.

Days morphed into weeks — then months. Nothing numbed the pain. Memories haunted Josh in bits and pieces. He recoiled again from Rachel's touch — food lost its flavor — thoughts of ending his life plagued him. He wanted to be free of the pain at any cost.

I remember wondering if anything could dull the pain. I longed to go home — not just to the States — I wanted to be safe and secure in my childhood home — to hear Pa's deep voice reading God's Word. I wanted to smell Ma's good cooking and hear the crackling logs in the open fireplace. I longed to feel the comfort of Ma's arms and hear her soothing voice telling me everything would be okay. I would have been horrified if I had known what was ahead.

Josh heard some folks found ways to cope when things were too hard to deal with. Some suggested Michael. He helped people forget.

Stumbling into Michael's tent Josh upset his nightstand — a lamp and table crashed to the ground. He mumbled an apology. Michael seemed a bit startled by his entrance but he had a look on his face like nothing surprised him. He had seen desperate men before.

"What can I do for you, buddy?"

"I need help."

Michael had access to whatever was needed. He was the supplier of pornography, alcohol, opioids and more. He was glad to have another customer. His services weren't cheap.

"I just want to forget."

"Sure. We all do. I have the perfect thing for you." Michael handed Josh a magazine and a few pills. "Here, buddy. It's on the house."

Josh wondered where this had been all his life. The porn and opiates were more seductive than anything he had ever experienced. He felt safe — comfortable — numbed and protected from the pain and emptiness of his life. The cravings for pornography and opiates soon had him addicted. He had a harem of women and the chemical high was exhilarating.

Josh went to see Michael often.

The conflict between what he was seeing and doing, what he knew was morally right, was huge. Josh realized he was fantasizing over someone's daughter — the women he viewed might have been trafficked. His actions brought him deep shame — but he was hooked.

To make things worse, Rachel found the magazines. She already knew something wasn't right. The addiction hit her hard.

MANHUNT

Josh had no idea the depth of grief, humiliation, hurt, rejection, and loneliness his selfish choices caused her.

Even though Rachel was beautiful she started to question her worth — wondered what was wrong with her — common among women who are sexually betrayed. None of it was her fault.

Josh promised to quit — but couldn't. His promises would last for a day or two — then he would succumb again. Porn was exciting. It delivered a lethal amount of euphoria from the hormone dopamine that keeps its prisoners shackled. It provided the excitement of tasting forbidden fruit and released him from all anxiety. It had the delicious excitement of secrecy and provided intense emotional bursts. It seemed good and evil at the same time. Josh was completely hooked.

The porn seemed to temporarily alleviate stress — but the guilt caused more stress. He was spiraling into a bottomless pit. His relationship with Rachel was empty — he didn't care. He just wanted to feel good. Porn became an escape from reality. It hid emotional scars, but didn't produce the same heady hit of endorphins Josh felt at first. The euphoria was gone. He wondered what else Michael had to offer.

Michael suggested a prostitute. Maybe that would provide more excitement? Michael had connections. It sounded enticing. Michael said it was discreet. No one would know. Josh never dreamed he'd go there but was being sucked into a black vortex. The pit got deeper and darker.

Josh dropped onto his cot.

He felt like he was sitting on the edge of a cliff and was about to fall over.

"I can't do life anymore."

Rachel sat on the cot across from him — wordlessly staring at him. He had changed so much she no longer knew him. They didn't get along at all. Rachel's words offended him easily so she usually said nothing.

"Life is meaningless. Nothing satisfies."

Josh took a deep breath then confessed, "I have been with prostitutes. I don't remember how many..."

If he had plunged a dagger deep into Rachel's heart, he couldn't have hurt her more. Josh ignored the pain in her eyes — thought his own pain was greater. She stared at him as tears welled. Her eyes asked, *"Who are you? How could you do this to me?"*

That's when Josh held out a handful of pills for inspection.

"See these? I'm going to kill the pain forever."

"What's your plan?" Rachel whispered. Now her eyes asked, *"How could this be my husband? Who is this man? Did I ever know him?"*

"First, I'm going to write my parents a goodbye letter..."

Staring out the open doorway — Josh lit a cigarette — then slowly turned and looked towards his wife. "I'm packing up my stuff to give away. I'll take the pills tonight."

Rachel tried to sound calm as she whispered, "I need to get some air."

Major Cook, the Commanding Officer, was startled to see Rachel burst into his tent. It was obvious by her wild eyes she had been crying — something was very wrong. He spoke as calmly as possible, "Good evening, Dr. Williams. What brings you to my little corner of the base?"

"Captain Williams is planning suicide! Permission to intervene, Sir."

"Suicide? Seriously? I thought he was recovering."

"He was getting better but relapsed. He has enough opiates to kill a platoon and plans to take them tonight, Sir."

"What's your proposal, Dr. Williams?"

"Sedation and immediate transport to the army's psychiatric hospital in Landstuhl, Germany, Sir."

"Could he be helped if he stayed here?"

"No, Sir. He needs 24/7 surveillance and full-time clinical help. That kind of support is not available here, Sir."

"Permission granted."

"Thank you, Sir."

"What are his chances?"

"This might save his life. Permission to have four men assist with the evacuation, Sir."

"Permission granted. I will summon a pilot and arrange for an immediate transport."

"Thank you, Sir."

"Where were you, Rachel? Why are these men standing in our tent?"

"They're here to help you, Josh."

"I don't need help! Y'all get out of my tent!"

"Josh, don't be belligerent."

"Don't tell me what to do!"

"You don't need to throw things all over the tent, Josh."

"I'll do what I like with my stuff!"

"It looks like a bomb went off here. What are you doing?"

"What do you think I'm doing? I'm packing up my stuff. I told you. Don't you listen?"

"Men, help!"

"Let go of me!"

"Men, hold him."

"A needle? What are you doing, Rachel?"

"Josh has been sedated and subdued. He is on a plane getting ready for take-off to the hospital, Sir."

"Excellent, Dr. Williams. Have the papers been sent?"

"Yes, Sir. They went with the accompanying officer. I filled them out before transport."

"I'm sorry, Dr. Williams. This must be very difficult for you."

Rachel suddenly felt light-headed and could barely stand.

"Rachel, are you okay?"

"No, Sir. I haven't been okay since Josh's last mission to the Kandahar mountains."

"That was a rough mission. Take some time off, Rachel. Let me know when you're ready to report back for duty."

"Thank you, Sir."

Rachel composed herself long enough to call Josh's parents — then slumped over her laptop to draft the most difficult letter she ever had to write. She rewrote it several times to try to get the wording just right.

> *Dear Josh,*
>
> *By the time you get this letter you will be at the psychiatric hospital in Germany. I am sorry you had to be sent there but there really were no other options. As you know, your life was spiraling out of control and you were in extreme danger.*
>
> *I am grieved over the choices you have made. I cannot live with your addictions. I don't know how we got here. At this time, I don't know if there is a future for us.*
>
> *I called your parents. They asked me to tell you they are praying for you. They don't know all the details. If you want them to know you can tell them.*
>
> *I hope for your recovery,*
> *Rachel*

All reports from the hospital were brief and not at all encouraging. Finally, after nearly a year, a report was placed on Rachel's desk. The envelope was sealed with 'CLASSIFIED REPORT' emblazoned across it.

CLASSIFIED REPORT

To: Dr. Rachel Williams
Kandahar Army Base, Afghanistan
From: Dr. Schmidt,
MD, PhD., LCSW, MFT
Army Substance Abuse Program
LRMC Landstuhl Psychiatric Hospital,
Germany

Dear Dr. Williams,

As you are aware, Captain Joshua Williams has been my patient for the past year. It was wise you initiated the process of having him sent here for treatment for his suicidal tendencies aggravated by PTSD and addictions. From my observations it is likely he would not have survived if he had stayed in Afghanistan. After assessments the medical team found the following:

1. *<u>Physiologically</u>, his body had a difficult time with normal physical activities. The first six months were spent fighting everyone he was in contact with at the hospital. Restraints had to be used several times to prevent him harming himself or others. He was belligerent and uncooperative with the entire medical team including myself, the social workers, the nurses, the neurologists, and the psychologists.*

2. *<u>Psychologically</u>, his mind and emotions appeared to be irreparably damaged. He had a difficult time being at the hospital and tried to escape several times. Captain Williams exhibited extreme paranoia and dissociation. He was mentally disconnected from his thoughts, feelings, surroundings and memories. His sense of identity was deeply affected by his attempts to lower his fears, trauma, anxiety and shame.*

3. *<u>Neurologically</u>, his nervous system responded to many triggers. We were unsure if there would be any success in helping him overcome the triggers that spawned his antisocial behaviors.*

> 4. <u>Psychotherapy</u>, *which should have helped, became a place for outbursts of rage and abusive behavior. This was unfortunate, as had he been willing to work with the medical team he might have improved sooner.*
>
> *This may sound completely bizarre, not scientific or professional at all. The change in Captain William's behavior has been astounding. The medical team has never encountered such an apparently hopeless case having such a drastic turn around in a matter of months. There is no explanation as to what has brought about this change. Captain Williams laughingly told us maybe God is answering his Pa's prayers.*
>
> *Therapists have counselled him on recovery techniques such as TRE (Tension Relaxing Exercises), and because he is accepting their advice, we are seeing daily improvements. Accepting a regular routine has helped immensely. Physical care has helped in his fight against addictions. When he is hungry, angry, lonely, bored or tired he needs to be vigilant as he is most vulnerable for relapse then. The triggers aren't affecting him at present. He has been given strategies to block the triggers and temptations that come into his mind and is developing new, healthy neural paths for his thoughts.*
>
> *The medical team is in favor of Captain William's release. He has an accountability partner who encourages him when there are temptations or relapses. This partner has committed to continue the accountability relationship after Captain Williams leaves the hospital. Please advise when you will be available for a follow-up assessment. It will ultimately be our mutual decision as to when he is released.*
>
> *Sincerely,*
> *Dr. Schmidt,*
> *MD, PhD, LCSW,*
> *MFT*

It seemed too good to be true.
Was Josh really better?
Family and friends advised her to leave the relationship.

"You're an idiot to stay."
"The man you married no longer exists."
"He is a broken shell of a man."
"You could save yourself a pile of grief if you walked away."
"Don't be a fool. A leopard never changes their spots."
"Once an addict always an addict."
"Just get rid of the bum!"

So many voices — it was tempting to walk away. Life would be much simpler. Contradictory emotions played in her heart. As a doctor she understood Josh's desperation to forget his pain. As a woman she knew in her heart the choices he made had nothing to do with her — yet it was difficult to be compassionate because she was wrapped up in her own hurt. Rachel realized she couldn't make any life-altering decisions in the throes of betrayal trauma. Her heart hoped there would be a light at the end of this dark tunnel — she still loved Josh — but she was afraid. She didn't want to be hurt again. Her professional training reminded her people could recover. There was hope.

The time in Kandahar had been beautiful and brutal at the same time. Rachel just wanted to see Josh and go home. Her mother suggested they come to New York City and figure things out before deciding what to do next. Rachel hoped she would be able to go home with Josh — but the future was uncertain.

The application to go to Germany was immediately filled out and delivered to the Commanding Officer. Rachel requested a release from the army. She had signed up for two years and had fulfilled the commitment. The final requested destination was New York City.

Rachel didn't dare tell her mother what happened with Josh. She was sure her mother would be heartbroken and would advise her to leave him — she was so protective of her only child. Becky only knew about the PTSD.

Rachel's visit to Landstuhl Psychiatric Hospital was hopeful. After discussions with Dr. Schmidt and the medical team Rachel met with Josh.

"Rachel," Josh spoke quietly. "I really do love you. I am so sorry I wasn't stronger for you — for us. I am sorry I put you through so much pain. Please forgive me."

Rachel felt hopeful. He sounded like the old Josh — kind, loving, compassionate. She decided at that moment to forgive — to give them a chance.

"I forgive you, Josh." Rachel knew when you forgive someone you release a prisoner — yourself. She had seen what bitterness and unforgiveness did to some of her patients. It wasn't pretty. Unforgiveness could easily destroy one's soul. She chose not to go there.

"Thank you. I'm grateful we have this chance to start over. The past two years have been painful. The hospital was a challenge — but it was necessary for me to find my way back to you."

"Josh, I'm hoping for a reset for us — a new beginning."

They had no idea the depth of despair both had been in — grief hit them hard as they cried in each other's arms. Repairing the brokenness would take courage — determination — they were both so emotionally fragile. Was wholeness possible? Rachel wasn't sure if their marriage could be renewed and their hearts healed. She didn't know if they could build trust again — but she believed everyone deserves a second chance.

The papers were signed for Josh's release. Flights were arranged to New York City.

"Josh, do you remember the saying I mentioned to you about a deep pit?"

"I don't."

"There is no pit so deep, that God's love is not deeper still."

"I don't think God's love reaches into the pit of Hell."

"True. That was written by a woman who had been in a concentration camp. She had been in a deep pit and felt God's love holding her. Do you think we need God now? Do you think He's answering our parents' prayers?"

"I don't believe we need God. We can handle this."
I can't believe how proud, arrogant — just plain stupid I was to think at that time we didn't need God. We needed Him desperately.

Rachel gazed out the window as the plane prepared for take-off. Germany had been a place of trial for Josh — but also a place of seemingly miraculous healing. Still — nagging thoughts crept into her mind. Was she being delusional — hoping for something impossible? Was Josh really better or was this an act to get out of the hospital? Did he really love her? Was he really sorry? Their marriage had been broken by PTSD, porn, prostitutes, alcohol and opioid addictions. Life had become surreal. Was she being deceived now by Josh's show of remorse and kindness? Was the pain really behind them? Rachel couldn't help wondering — was Josh really well? Did he secretly still desire his addictions? How much could she believe?

She loved Josh but all trust in him was shattered. In spite of her fears and misgivings — Rachel was looking forward to taking him home to her Mama in New York City.

Josh reached across the airplane tray to hold her hand. The look of remorse on his face was real. "Honey, I don't ever want to hurt you again."

The loving, kind man she fell in love with did seem to be back. "I'm glad you're better, Josh."

"Honey, my Pa will want to give God thanks and say it was an answer to prayer. Just you wait. He believes all that God stuff."

"I'm excited to meet your Ma and Pa. They sound wonderful."

The barn quieted down for the night. Josh was lulled to sleep by a barn cat purring by his ear. He thought about that trip to America. *We had no idea how bittersweet the days ahead would be.*

Sweet Home Alabama

"God sets the lonely in families..."
Psalm 68:6

MANHUNT

Josh's stomach growled. There was nothing to eat in the barn except gruesome looking pig slop. He decided to ignore the pangs gnawing at his gut. Watching the sun sparkle in the dust particles above his head, random scenes from his life continued to meander through his mind.

So much happened once they were been back in the States. Was it really already seven years ago they arrived in New York City? What an incredible time that had been. Rachel's forgiveness was total. She was an incredible woman — never brought up the past — maybe she was worried if she reminded Josh of anything frightening he might be triggered and spiral into darkness again.

Rachel's Mom Becky was a godly woman. They tried calling her after the disappearance but could never get hold of her.

Becky was shocked when she met Josh in Afghanistan at the wedding. She marveled at how much Josh looked like Rachel's dad. Was Rachel attracted to him because of that? Rachel had seen photos of her dad when she was young — but the pictures had been discarded years ago. Becky couldn't bear to have them around — reminded her too much of what could have been.

Did Rachel have a subconscious memory of the man in the photos? Rachel's dad was a tall, handsome man with thick, dark hair and dazzling, hazel eyes — just like Josh. They had the same charming smile. Becky hoped that was all they had in common.

Becky's husband had been a drinker and a womanizer. His involvement with the mob and prostitution made him the object of a nation-wide manhunt. Becky wasn't sure exactly what he had done. Whatever the crime was, it was obviously horrendous. All she knew was his crime landed him in jail for life. Becky didn't have the heart to tell her daughter. Rachel assumed he was in New York City somewhere and not at all interested in meeting her.

Becky visited him once after he was locked up in prison. It was to say goodbye. Her husband told her he had lined up for a second serving of delicious bread in the prison cafeteria. A guard hauled him out of line and berated him yelling, "What do ya think you're doing? You know prisoners are only allowed in the line once. Get outta here!"

Rachel's dad wept as he quoted a Scripture. It had perplexed him since he was a boy. He finally understood the meaning.

"For a prostitute reduces you to a piece of bread.
The adulteress hunts for your precious life."
Proverbs 6:26

He cried as he told her he was sorry he hurt her — heartbroken he had made such a mess of his life. Becky said she forgave him but told him this was goodbye. She hadn't seen her husband in over twenty years. Becky would have been horrified if she knew the truth about Josh — that he had made similar choices.

Josh had never explored a big city before so he wandered around like a kid in a candy store. He bought a camera and photographed everything.

"Josh, what're you going to do with so many photos?"

"Keep them, of course," Josh grinned.

"I didn't know you loved photography."

There was so much they didn't know about each other. Sipping coffee for months in an Afghan coffee shop or sitting on the turret of a tank under the stars doesn't give you a picture of the whole person. So, it seemed like this was a time for getting to know each other in civilian life.

After two weeks in New York City they planned to visit Ma and Pa in Sheffield, Alabama — after that life was uncertain. That was a bit unsettling — they had no direction. While standing in Times Square there was an unexpected call. Thankfully Rachel was inspecting a statue and didn't overhear the conversation.

"What is it, Pa?"

"Take over the farm? But Pa..."

"Why? The farm is your life..."

"But you're still young enough to farm..."

Rachel heard the worried tone in Josh's voice. She was going to walk over but Josh motioned for her to stay back.

"Yes...look after Ma? Naturally. But why, Pa?"

"Of course, I promise not to sell the farm."

Rachel could see the troubled look on Josh's face. She wanted to stand by him — but respected his wish to have her stand at a distance.

"I can't tell Ma or Rachel?"

"Cancer?" Josh whispered, "Final stages?"

Pa told Josh he decided to forego chemotherapy. Pa didn't want anyone but Josh knowing — he wanted life to be normal for as long as possible.

"Thank you, Pa. I love you too."

Pa only told Josh because he needed his consent to see a lawyer to transfer ownership of the farm. He knew Josh would take good care of his Emily.

Josh walked over to Rachel.

"That was Pa."

"What did he say?"

Josh didn't care they were in the middle of Times Square — didn't care if people stared at them. He hugged Rachel and sobbed.

When he could finally speak Josh said, "Rachel, dad just offered us his farm."

"Why are you crying? What is it you're not telling me, Josh?"

"I promised Pa not to tell you. You'll find out soon enough."

It was a bittersweet moment. He was thankful for Pa's kindness — but devastated by the news.

The ferry to Ellis Island to see the Statue of Liberty was a photographer's dream. They were surprised to learn nearly twelve million immigrants to America had once passed through Ellis Island — the nation's busiest immigration station.

"Josh, I think the 'staircase of separation' must have been a sad place."

"Why?"

"Immigrants lined up to be inspected there. If a doctor thought something was wrong with someone they would be deported back to where they came from. It must have been a place of dashed dreams for many."

"I can't imagine how terrible that must have been," Josh added.

Josh thought the Empire State Building was glorious to see. There was an incredible view of six states from the lookout on the 86th floor. That's when Josh discovered Rachel was afraid of heights.

The *New York Harbor Lights Evening Cruise* down the Hudson River and up the East River was romantic but not at all what they expected. "Josh, this cruise is cool — but it's too bad the windows are so foggy. It's hard to see anything. I wanted to see the city by night."

"No worries. Let's go on the deck."

Rachel wrapped her coat tightly around her as a shield from the biting wind. Josh was so excited to get photos of the New York City skyline at night he was oblivious to the cold.

"Darling, if you love photography so much, why didn't you take photos in Kandahar?"

"Photos were forbidden, Honey. Only photojournalists and war correspondents were allowed to take pictures. I could have been court-martialed. There were so many top-secret missions it would have been extremely dangerous to pull out a camera."

"Oh, I had no idea."

The next day, Josh lamented to his mother-in-law, "We only have two weeks here! There's so much to see and do!"

Becky laughed. "You must come visit me at the Metropolitan Museum of Art. I'll give you one of my world-famous tours."

"Becky, you must love working here! Thanks for this tour."

"Josh, this is the third most visited art museum in the world. There is a permanent collection of paintings and sculptures from nearly every European master," Becky informed them.

"That's amazing. Rachel, just look at the American and modern art exhibits!"

Rachel had no idea Josh knew so much about art. He almost could have joined Becky as a guide at the museum.

"Josh, look at this Islamic art! It's fascinating." Rachel felt like the art was a window into the soul of the people she had come to love in Afghanistan.

They were both filled with excitement as they explored this intriguing city. The more time they spent together the more his heart filled with love for his precious wife. He had never felt so much joy in all his life. How could she be so loving and forgiving? Why had he been such an idiot?

When Rachel held his hand to lead Josh to her favorite places they both felt electricity as their fingers touched. Their marriage was not only being restored it was being transformed into something special. The intensity and depth of their connection surprised them.

"Rachel, let's go on a buggy tour of Central Park. That poor horse looks bored just standing there."

"I'd love to. I've never gone on a buggy ride before."

"That was the fastest forty-five-minutes. There was so much to see it seemed like moments," Josh said.

"There's so many cool things to see. Let's walk the buggy route to see everything we passed."

"Great idea!"

Harlem Meer was a lovely little pond. Fishing poles and bait were available at the nearby Discovery Center. "Rachel, you trying to fish is the most hilarious thing I've ever seen." Josh stopped laughing when she reeled in a huge bass.

"I came to Central Park as a child with my mother. We skated on Wollman Lake in the winter and rowed on it in the summers. Mom took me to the Dana Discovery Center on weekends — they had a year-round educational program. She wanted me to have lots of opportunities. She said she wanted me to have a better life than she had — never explained what she meant. My mother always worried about me."

Rachel was positive there was nothing new for her to see in Central Park. She was quite surprised she had never heard of Belvedere Castle.

"Rachel. Just look at this castle! What great views! This deck is perfect for photos."

Rachel was thrilled Josh enjoyed her city. It was exhilarating being with him — he wanted to do everything!

"Let's go on a tour of all the boroughs — Brooklyn, Bronx, Harlem, Queens and Coney Island. It's only a seven-hour coach trip! I'm sure it'll be worth it," Josh exclaimed.

"Seven hours? You're kidding, right?"

"The sign says it's that long — if the traffic cooperates. Otherwise it's much longer," Josh grinned.

Josh was so excited Rachel couldn't say no. Francis, the tour guide, was hilarious. He tried to make the tour different from your usual run of the mill tours — entertaining as well as informing his delighted guests. Rachel thought he was a perfect stand-up comedian.

Nathan's famous hot dogs were a hit with Josh. He devoured four of them. The pigeons noticed the hotdogs and crowded around Josh's feet jockeying for the best position — hoping Josh would share bits with them. There seemed to be masses of hungry pigeons everywhere.

They took a yellow cab and stood admiring the Brooklyn Bridge.

"That bridge brings back so many memories. My Mom brought me here every Christmas Eve since I was a little girl to see the bridge all lit up. It was breathtaking — millions of lights were strewn across the suspension cables. Vendors sold us steaming cups of cocoa and bags of hot roasted chestnuts. Going to the bridge on Christmas Eve is a special holiday tradition for my mom and I."

"I'd love to see it at Christmas, Honey. Maybe we could come visit your mom then."

"I'm sure she'd be delighted to have us."

Josh loved the idea of coming back to this historical city. There was still so much to see. Josh repeated, "Two weeks is barely enough time to see the sights!"

Rachel laughed. "I know what you mean. I've lived here all my life and I'm still finding new places — can't believe I'd never heard of the 'Catacombs by Night'!"

"That was wild — walking in a one-hundred and fifty-year-old pipe organ. I had no idea those things were so massive. Thankfully no one began to play while we were inside," Josh laughed.

As they said goodbye to New York City Josh thanked Becky for the wonderful visit. "Thank you for everything, Ma'am. New York City's very special. I can see why you love it here."

"Maybe you could come visit at Christmas time? The city is transformed during the holidays."

"That would be terrific, Ma'am! We'd love to visit!"

"Josh, please call me 'Mom'."

"Okay, Mom."

As Josh grabbed their suitcases Rachel started to cry. "Bye, Mama. I love you. I miss you already. Come visit us in Alabama."

Becky cried as she hugged her daughter. "Let me know when the house is ready and I'll be there. Josh, please take care of my baby girl."

"I will, Mom. My Pa and Ma have always wanted a daughter. They are going to spoil her like crazy."

Tom's hayloft was a great place for thinking. Josh continued reminiscing about his farm — his little animal menagerie — the chickens, a couple bloodhounds, a horse, five sheep, and a one-eared cat. Boots had been rescued from a kill shelter in New York City about a year before Rachel went to Afghanistan. Poor Boots had lost most of an ear so she had a rather rough look. The neurotic cat yowled every time she was left alone too long — such separation anxiety — probably from being abandoned. She wanted her family in sight as much as possible.

The bloodhounds loved to bring dead coons and 'possums home and leave them lying on the back porch as a gift for the family. So thoughtful.

Their home was nestled on a hill by a mess of oaks and pecans. There was a backwater spot teeming with catfish and bass. Josh loved fishing there with his girls. Rachel taught Juliet how to make hush puppies — deep-fried cornmeal balls. They were great with fried catfish and bass.

There was a big ol' swing hanging from the oak near the river. Josh climbed that tree to be sure the gator couldn't reach him. That thought brought him back to his present reality. He was in Tom's barn — hungry, tired, cold, wounded. It was too much to think about. Overwhelming. He went back to his musings about the past. That kept him sane.

The garden was stunning when all the flowers were in bloom. It was a source of joy for Rachel to grow things. She didn't have a garden growing up in New York City. Flowers don't do well in concrete. The only thing left in her garden were the heirloom sunflowers nodding their heads full of seeds behind the little fence. Such exotic looking flowers with their vivid shades of purple, orange and scarlet.

Josh heard the cows lowing for food. He watched the fireflies flitting about his head. He was lulled to sleep by the lullaby of a cricket chorus.

MANHUNT

A bat flitting by his head searching for bugs woke Josh with a start. It was so close he felt the flapping of its wings by his face. He had been having a vivid dream about his Pa — didn't want to let the dream go so he replayed it.

When they spoke on the phone, Pa insisted on helping Josh and Rachel build a home. Arriving back at the farm, Josh was shocked to see how run-down things were. He and Pa worked together for months to get things running smoothly again. Thankfully Josh arrived in time to help plant crops — Pa wouldn't have had the energy to do that alone.

Josh could see Pa going downhill every day. He thought building a house would be too much for Pa, but he would not be deterred. Josh knew since he was a boy where he wanted to build his home one day — by his favorite oak and his best fishing hole.

Pa was a hero even though he was in pain. He worked hard — too hard.

"Josh, your parents are kind to let us stay with them. Your Pa is putting in such long hours to help build our house." Rachel couldn't stop talking about how loving Josh's folks were.

"Yes, they are the best."

The time with Ma and Pa was a time of deep healing. Rachel had never felt so loved.

Ma helped Rachel become an amazing Southern cook. Her fried chicken, black-eyed peas, cornbread, and of course, pecan pie, became famous.

Ma and Pa were kind people. They had lots of solid advice about marriage.

"Now, Josh. It's all about love and respect. Your best hope for your marriage to your pretty little wife is to love her. When she knows she's loved it's easier for her to respect you," Pa informed him as they laid out the foundations of the house.

"Like this here house. Y'all have to lay a good foundation in a marriage or the house will fall apart."

She hadn't had a dad since she was a little girl — so she adopted Pa as her very own. They would sit in front of the fireplace and talk for hours in the evenings. Pa whittled and shared whatever came into his heart to encourage his beloved daughter-in-law.

"Rachel, sometimes feelings can be fickle things. Choose to act lovingly even if you don't feel like it," Pa said.

"Rachel, all folks need affirming — need to know they are special to someone. To affirm someone, you have to know them," Ma advised.

"Y'all have to take time to understand one another's strengths. Then you can sound honest when you affirm them," Pa said.

Ma added, "Thankfulness and expressed gratitude are deeply romantic. A person feels seen and understood when they're appreciated."

Josh and Rachel often sat by the fireplace — sipping tea while listening to Ma and Pa's wise advice.

"Never take each other for granted. As time goes on people can feel taken for granted. You don't have to have a passionless relationship," Ma said as she smiled at Pa.

"Always look for ways to express your love to each other," Pa added as he leaned over and gave Ma a kiss.

"True," Josh replied. "Otherwise, a person can feel invisible to the people who are supposed to care about them."

Josh knew Rachel felt invisible for years. His heart was healing and he wanted Rachel's heart to heal too. He wanted his wife to know he was sorry he treated her so terribly for years — that she really was deeply valued and loved.

"The honeymoon doesn't ever have to end. It can keep getting better and better if folks don't let the relationship die," Pa said.

"What can I do, Pa?"

"Romance means meeting needs in your spouse."

"But how, Pa?"

"Well, I tried at some point every day to show my Emily how much I love her. I often pick flowers in the field for her or write her a note to tell her I love her. Don't you get lazy now and forget to tell your sweet wife every day she is the love of your life."

MANHUNT

Pa was the most loving man Rachel had ever met. No wonder Josh was a good man. He had a great example while growing up.

"Son, today I'm feeling a bit tired — working on the house has been hard. Why don't we sit under the willow a spell — Rachel brought us some of Ma's good sun tea and cookies."

"Okay Pa. It's awfully hot today. I could use a break." "Son, I want to tell you how glad I am you and Rachel are here. You know, my boy, your Ma and I prayed for you every day of your life — especially while you were in Afghanistan and Germany."

"Thanks, Pa."

"Josh — something's been on my heart for a while."

"What's that, Pa?"

"I've wondered over the years if your Ma and I taught you enough about God. You surely need Him, Son — we're living in stressful days."

"I know, Pa. I see it on the news. We're in crazy times."

"Well, Son, I want to make sure I've told you Jesus is real. Do you recall me telling you when you were a boy Jesus gave His life to pay for your sins?"

"Pa, I know I'm a sinner."

"Well, He's coming back —maybe real soon," Pa said. 'I know I'm going to Heaven to be with Him — I want you there too."

"I'll think about it, Pa."

"That's good, Son. Do you have a Bible?"

"Yes, I found one in Afghanistan."

"I sure hope you take the time to read it — especially the book of John."

"Maybe one day, Pa. I've seen some pretty bizarre stuff on Christian TV. It was nothing like I remember from church when I was a boy. I need to sort some of that out, Pa, cause if that's Christianity I'm not interested."

"What bothered you, Son?"

"Well Pa, I'm confused about some things I've heard and seen. You said there's a place called Hell. I heard folks say there is likely no such place as Hell. I heard folks say Jesus is never coming back. Others say there's no absolute truth — no faith or religion is true."

"Well Son, they must not have noticed John 14:6 in the Bible. *"Jesus said to him, "I am the way, the truth, and the life. No one comes to the Father, except through me.* That's a pretty clear statement. He is the only way to God. Period. All other routes are false."

"How do we know for sure, Pa? I've heard people say that's a pretty narrow statement."

"Josh, there can only be one truth. If Jesus said He is the Way and He is speaking truth, then all other ways are deceptions to lead people away from the narrow path."

"I'm just not convinced, Pa. I have so many questions."

"Josh, my time is short. I'd love to sit down with you sometime and go over your questions. Let me know when you're ready."

"I will, Pa."

We never had that chance...

"Josh, do you have time to sit a spell on the porch swing?"

"Why Rachel, Honey, you're sounding more like a Southern belle every day," Josh laughed as he plopped down on the swing.

"I noticed you sitting under the willow with Pa for quite a while today. It seemed like you were having a deep conversation."

"Pa was reminding me of my spiritual roots. He wants me to be in Heaven with him."

"He loves you, Josh."

"I know. Ma and Pa taught me about God since I was a boy. I was a good kid — respectful and all. I honored my parents

— believed in God with my head — but Christianity never got into my heart."

"My mom offered me a Bible but I told her I found one in Afghanistan," Rachel volunteered.

"I told Pa the same thing."

"I have to admit I have fond memories of attending Brooklyn Tabernacle as a girl. Children's Church was a lot of fun. The Youth Group was cool but when I was in my later teens I kind of gave up on Christianity. Mom still goes there faithfully — she loves Pastor Cymbala's preaching and his wife's music."

"Rachel, what made you turn your back on God?"

"Part of the reason is because so many of my friends went to church's I thought were wacky."

"What do you mean?"

"My mom was so glad I finally found Christian friends. She would have been shocked if she knew their beliefs. Janie used Destiny cards — basically tarot cards for Christians — to give me "prophetic messages". She seemed to value experiences more than the Bible. She loved Bethel Church. Their pastor wrote a book claiming the things of the New Age were stolen from God and had to be reclaimed. Janie believed him. So weird. I thought it was absurd people thought witchcraft and occult devices were from God."

"Where did they get such crazy ideas?"

"I have no idea. Mom said some pastors taught doctrines of demons and I had to be careful — or I could be deceived. I didn't dare tell her about my friends. It seemed all my so-called Christian friends were into strange teachings."

"Like what else?"

"Well — Jessie thought lying on graves of deceased saints to soak up their spirits — grave soaking — was a great idea. I thought it was creepy my friends wanted to hang out in cemeteries to soak up spirits of dead people."

"That does sound disturbing, Rachel."

"Carol — another friend from school — invited me to her "New Apostolic Reformation" NAR church. They have a teaching called Dominion Theology that says all of society will be under Christian dominion. They believe the church will present a perfect world to Christ when He returns. Sounds like wishful thinking to me."

"I can't imagine."

"Chrissy took me to her "Postmodern-Emergent" church. They emphasized experiences over the Bible. Often the Bible wasn't even mentioned and experiences or articles from newspapers were discussed in the messages. They said the Bible was just interesting stories. I took my mom to one of their church services. She said it reminded her of a laser light rock concert — she didn't think God was being worshipped. Not like Brooklyn Tabernacle."

"Ma and Pa wouldn't like that, either — could be cause they're older and they are used to singing from a hymn book."

"Mom hoped for the longest time I would go to Bible School and marry a pastor. She's the one who decided I shouldn't go when she found out they taught the Word of God couldn't be trusted — the Bible was mostly interesting stories. Students were told the garden of Eden, the devil, and Hell were just allegories — stories or myths to reveal moral truths."

"Who has the authority to decide what is truth?" Josh wondered.

"That's a good question. I have no idea. The more I saw of Christianity the more I thought it was weird — definitely not for me. None of the churches I visited with my friends seemed real. It was like there was something huge missing. I think it was the God Pastor Cymbala talked about. I didn't realize that until just now."

"Crazy experiences, Rachel. Thankfully, I didn't see any weird stuff. Pa loves Charles Stanley's and Dr. David Jeremiah's teachings. He says they are such godly men — great evangelists and Bible teachers. Solid. Pa said thousands became followers of Jesus because of them. He loved telling me about their teachings."

"My Mom likes them, too."

He also respects the teachings of J. D. Farag, Jan Markell, Billy Crone, and Jack Hibbs. Pa asked me several times if I wanted to accept Christ but I just never could see why I needed God. My life was fine without Him."

"Do you think we need God now, Josh?"

"Not now. Maybe one day. We'll see."

They were only at Ma and Pa's for a couple months when it was discovered they were expecting a baby. Such incredible joy! If Rachel felt pampered before, it was nothing compared to how she felt now. She wasn't allowed to carry slop to the pigs anymore or pails of corn to the chickens. She told Josh she felt like a princess.

"Rachel, sit yourself down, girl. Rest. Have some sun tea," Ma said.

Taking lunch to the men — admiring their work — sitting by the river watching the little house being built — was about all the exercise she was allowed.

The house was close to Ma and Pa's — which was a comfort. Ma had been a nurse and planned to help with the delivery. All Josh had to do was holler out the back door and Ma would be there in moments.

"Josh, I'm so thankful your Pa invited you and Rachel to move here. I'm looking forward to being a mid-wife for my precious daughter-in-love and our grand-baby."

It seemed like the baby and the house were both ready almost at the same time. They barely moved in when Josh was hollering for the mid-wife. Ma came running with all the things she had prepared.

"Now Josh, you go keep Pa company. I'll call if I need you."

Ma was soon hollering from the back door for the men to come meet baby Juliet Becky Emily. They all thought she was the most perfect baby ever. They marvelled over her tiny, perfect fingers, toes, fingernails, sparkling blue eyes — everything.

"Well, Rachel, you're gonna need a good fireplace to keep my little grand-sugar warm in the winter. How'd you like a river rock one?"

Rachel loved the rock fireplace in Ma and Pa's home.

"Sounds lovely, Pa."

The men got to work hauling rocks. The fireplace was nearly built when Rachel realized Pa wasn't well. His breathing seemed labored...

"Pa, you're working too hard. Are you okay? Maybe you should rest?"

"I'm fine, Rachel. I want to get these last rocks in place. I want my girls to be warm this winter."

That was the last thing Pa ever said. He sat down for a moment and never got up. Actually, the real Pa got up and stepped into eternity.

Rachel was so startled she started to scream, "JOSH!"

Rushing in — Josh tried CPR — too late. Pa was already in Heaven. Rachel dropped on the sofa and sobbed. The noise startled Juliet, who started to scream. Rachel rocked her baby girl as she held her close. Mommy and baby cried together.

"Rachel, Pa didn't tell you. He had cancer. You being here brought great joy to his last days — he didn't want you to fret. Ma, you and our baby girl were the joy of his life."

Rachel cried uncontrollably. Josh held her and baby Juliet close as he continued.

"He'd want me to tell you he loved you like a daughter. He was so proud of how you looked after his little granddaughter. It's funny how he loved to call her his little grand-sugar."

How could they ever tell Ma? Josh called emergency services and informed them of Pa's death.

"Ma, could you come over, please?" Josh asked Ma on the phone. When Ma saw the emergency vehicles she ran. Coming in the door Ma saw Rachel in a heap of sorrow.

"Was it Pa?"

Josh threw his arms around his Ma and held her close.

Time seemed to stand still — it has a funny way of doing that when things are surreal. The ticking of the clock on the mantle sounded abnormally loud and everything else abnormally quiet. Ma's sobs finally subsided.

"He had cancer, Ma. He didn't want you to know. He wanted you to be happy."

"I knew, Josh. Somehow, I knew."

Many folks got up to share at Pa's funeral.

"He encouraged and inspired others."

"He was a kind, loving man."

"He was the Pa I never had. I loved him deeply," Rachel sobbed.

Ma spoke up, "Did y'all all know Pa was in a terrible car accident about seventeen years ago? He nearly died. God showed him a vision of people on their way to Heaven. God turned him around and showed him the people behind him and informed him he could be with God then if he wanted or he could stay for the ones behind him. He chose to stay. He must have seen y'all. God knew y'all needed him."

People sobbed.

"Pa was a good man. He had so much wisdom."

"He loved people."

"He was a man of integrity."

"Cared deeply for the needs of others."

"When he gave his word, it was a solemn promise that'd never be broken."

I'm so thankful for my Pa," Josh shared. "Every day for forty years Pa left a note or flowers on the table before he went to work at the mine to let my Ma know he loved her. He was the most loving man I have ever known."

They buried Pa next to his favorite willow by the river. Ma could be seen there in the mornings reading her Bible. The townsfolk were sorry to see such a fine man die so young. He was only sixty-seven.

It was suggested Ma move in with Josh's family so she could be taken care of — but she wanted no part of that notion. She was fiercely independent like her son. She loved the little house her husband built for her. Ma planned to stay there as long as she could keep the fireplace going.

She lived by herself — until the day of the disappearance. That was the last day they saw Ma.

The years rolled by. Because Josh had been honorably discharged for medical reasons from the Marines, he had a Veteran's pension—it enabled them to live comfortably. The pension helped as the crops weren't always a reliable source of income. Rachel's little garden and the chickens provided much of their food.

Juliet was a precocious child — started reading at five. Now that she was seven years old she loved taking stacks of books and lying in front of the fireplace to read them. She knew Grandpa built it special for her.

"Mama, can you tell me more stories about Grandpa and Grandma?"

Juliet knew her Grandparents from all she heard about them. She loved being told Grandpa called her his little grand-sugar — loved the story about how Grandma was with her when she was born. Juliet was blissfully happy with what she thought was the best Daddy and Mama on earth.

My precious Juliet, you would have been horrified to know how your life was about to change.

Josh realized his time in the barn would have to end soon. If he didn't find food he would be too weak to try to escape the Manhunters.

The Witnesses

*"But you will receive power when the
Holy Spirit has come upon you.
You will be witnesses to me in Jerusalem,
in all Judea and Samaria,
and to the uttermost parts of the earth."
Acts 1:8*

Standing on a high mountain — in the exact spot an ancient prophet once called down fire from Heaven — Josh watched as a cloud of fire surged towards him. It was a fearful sight but he felt no fear.

The cloud pulsated with power.

A mighty wind whirled around him.

Was he awake or asleep? Was this a vision or a dream?

He understood things he shouldn't have known. He had never been there before — yet he knew he was standing on Mount Carmel in Israel. He knew this was the spot where Elijah had called out the prophets of Baal.

A mighty tongue of fire leaped out of the cloud and blazed above him.

As it touched his head the flame surged through his body but he felt no heat.

He felt the power of God and was filled with the Holy Spirit. He began speaking a language he didn't know. Was it Hebrew?

Josh realized this was what the prophet Joel foretold would happen in the last days of earth.

> *"It will happen afterward,*
> *that I will pour out my Spirit on all flesh;*
> *and your sons and your daughters will prophesy.*
> *Your old men will dream dreams.*
> *Your young men will see visions."*
> *Joel 2:28*

Men walked out of the flames — a few at a time — slowly building to thousands. The fire ignited them — their spirits came alive with the anointing and power of God.

Four angels stood ready to unleash God's judgement on earth. A fifth angel stopped them. They had to wait until these 144,000 men — 12,000 from each tribe of Israel — were sealed with the name of God on their foreheads.

Would the seal protect them from the wrath to come? Perhaps it was a sign to all of the empowerment of the Ruach Hakodesh

— God's powerful Holy Spirit. Fingers of fire leaped out of the cloud and emblazoned the Name of God on each forehead.

Without being told — Josh knew these men were virgins — not caught up with the cares of this life. They had no earthly attachments to keep them back from total allegiance to the LORD — to the Lamb — and followed wherever He led. They could freely share the love of God. They needed this freedom to stay ahead of the Manhunters.

Josh watched as the 144,000 scattered to the four winds — with hearts on fire for God — prepared to take His gospel message to a rebellious world.

Josh awoke — still in the hayloft. So — it was a dream. Josh recognized God could easily have abandoned the people of earth after the disappearance. He could have called the rebellious ones fools and turned His back on them — but He didn't. He refused to leave people without a chance to turn to Him.

Pa had said it's not God's will for any to perish but for all to come to repentance. Because of the hardness of his heart — his stupidity in not listening to Pa — Josh now faced the dangerous days of the Tribulation. He had prevented Rachel from turning to Christ. What a complete idiot he had been. Would they survive? He knew they had to be strong.

He lay back in the hay thinking about God's grace and mercy. Dozing — Josh was uncertain if he was asleep or awake. He saw a shoreline filled with massive boulders. A man stood high on a rock — swinging a bright lantern into the night sky so those who were caught in the swirling dark waters below could make their way to shore. He realized with surprise the man was Jesus — scanning the deep, raging sea of humanity — searching for all who were lost. He couldn't intervene — people had to be free to choose or reject Him. If He interfered — He would violate the free will choice He had given all mankind. Josh saw His arm extended — reaching out to rescue all who turned to Him. He heard God pleading with the masses of drowning souls,

MANHUNT

"Come to Me...I will loose the bands of wickedness...I will undo the heavy burdens... the oppressed will go free...every yoke will be broken...I am the Way, the Truth, the Life..."

There was anguish on God's face as He saw many swept under the waves — lost to Him for all eternity. Josh looked at the people struggling in the waves. Blinders were over their eyes. Their hearts were hardened — their ears couldn't hear God calling. They couldn't see they were the prey of a terrible dark lord whose goal was to destroy them.

Josh realized he had been one of those hard-hearted, drowning souls. The day he reached for that outstretched arm and left the black waters forever was burned in his memory.

That day, a news report flashed across the TV screen. He hated to disturb Rachel — she was busy making his favorite pecan pie — but she *had* to see this.

"Rachel, Honey. Come quick!"

"What is it, Josh?"

"There are two guys who say they are God's prophets standing in the street in Jerusalem."

"Why?"

"They are calling people to repent. They are the ones that held back the rain for so long. Look at them, Rachel."

"They look wild — like Old Testament prophets might have looked — dressed in sackcloth — long beards — wild hair."

"Shhh. The news reporter is commenting."

"Good evening, folks. This is Stan Hobbs — coming to you live from Jerusalem on World Wide News. We're here to cover the story of two men calling themselves "The Two Witnesses". They claim to be prophets of God. Let's listen."

"THE WRATH OF GOD IS ABOUT TO FALL ON EARTH!"

"There you have it folks. These delusional men are warning the world the wrath of God is about to fall on earth. Have you ever heard anything so ridiculous?"

"UNLESS YOU REPENT YOU WILL LIKEWISE PERISH!"

"They are saying people must repent or they will perish. Sounds crazy to me. Repent from what?"

"REPENT — FOR THE KINGDOM OF HEAVEN IS AT HAND!"

"Okay folks, there's a crowd gathering. It looks like a riot! Some are picking up rocks to throw at the insane "Witnesses". This is looking nasty!"

"Josh, the Witnesses look like there's fire in their eyes."
"I know. They seem to be lit up with power. Just watch, Honey. You aren't going to believe this. Fire is going to come out of their mouths."
"What? That sounds a bit far-fetched, Josh. Why do you think that?"
"If these are the two witnesses the Bible talks about — you'll see fire."
"Josh, just look at the crowd mocking those two men."
"They better stop or they'll be sorry. The last time anyone mocked Elijah a bear mauled a crowd."
"JOSH!!! I can't believe what I just saw! Did you see that?"
"Unbelievable! Fire came out of their mouths and devoured the crowd!"

"They're gone! The crowd's gone!!! Even the news reporter's missing! I can't believe it! Josh, how did you know THAT was going to happen?"

"Revelation 11 said fire would come out of the mouths of the two witnesses and devour their enemies. I figured these could be the guys."

"What on earth! Who are these men?"

"Maybe Enoch and Elijah? They never died. I read in the Bible it's appointed unto man once to die. Enoch was so righteous he walked with God on earth and then walked right into Heaven. Elijah was taken up in a whirlwind — in a fiery chariot — straight into Heaven. Maybe one the prophets is Moses? My vote is any of those three could be standing there."

"Josh, I'm scared."

"Honey, look! Now the camera is showing a close up of the witnesses commanding the heavens to be shut up so there's no rain on the earth. The Bible says they would say that. I think the last droughts were just build ups. They are saying it's not going to rain now for three and a half years."

"I'm really scared, Josh."

"They said God is giving people time to repent."

"Josh, people won't repent. You know that. Three and a half years — how will the earth survive without rain?"

"That's not all, Rachel. The Bible says these men are going to turn water into blood — and release plagues on mankind."

"Oh man. Reminds me of Moses in Egypt."

"Definitely seems the same."

"Josh, this sounds terrifying."

"It does. Oh — I found a letter Pa left in his Bible for us."

"What's it say, Josh?"

"I haven't had a chance to read it yet. I'll go grab it. Be right back…"

Dearest Josh and Rachel,

If you are reading these words, I am gone. Please give my precious little grand-sugar a hug for me and tell Juliet I love her. Words are inadequate to say how much I love y'all.

I am deeply sorry you are not with Ma and I — I cannot imagine the fear that has come on the earth. These events have been known by God since the foundation of the world. He has graciously left a window open for you to accept Him as your Lord and Savior. That window may close quickly. This letter may be your last invitation to be part of God's forever family.

God said there would be a Rapture and if you are reading this — it's happened — just as He foretold thousands of years ago. The true church — the followers of Jesus Christ — are gone.

> *"For the Lord himself will descend*
> *from Heaven with a shout,*
> *with the voice of the archangel*
> *and with God's trumpet.*
> *The dead in Christ will rise first, then*
> *we who are alive, who are left,*
> *will be caught up together with them in*
> *the clouds, to meet the Lord in the air.*
> *So we will be with the Lord forever."*
> *1 Thessalonians 4:16-17*

I'm going to be very frank with you in this letter. You are in dire straits — a time of great peril — and what I am about to tell you is your only way to be strong and survive this terrible time.

The world must be spinning in chaos right now since the disappearance of millions of people. No matter what you have been told — trust God. He loves you more than you could possibly imagine. You may hear some crazy things — like aliens removed all the Christians so the enlightened folk of earth could evolve to the next level. Whatever you've been told — if it's not in the Bible — don't believe it. Hang on to the truth of God's Word. Your eternal soul depends on it.

The cup of iniquity has been filled and God has said "Enough!" The goodness that restrained the devil's evil has been removed. God is about to pour out judgement. Mankind has foolishly hardened their hearts against God — so He is about to send a powerful delusion on those who rejected Him. If you do not repent and accept Jesus as your Savior — you won't be able to resist the deception — you will believe the lies. Once this happens, all folks who rejected Christ will be lost forever.

> *"...God sends them a working of error,*
> *that they should believe a lie;*
> *that they might be judged who*
> *didn't believe the truth,*
> *but had pleasure in unrighteousness."*
> 2 Thessalonians 2:11

I wrote notes in the margins of my Bible for you. Genesis talks about a rebellion in Heaven. I don't know how much of this you recall from my reading the Bible to you when you were a boy — so I'll refresh your memory. Here are the highlights.

There was a rebellion in Heaven. The time-line is uncertain — we don't know when the rebellion happened or when God created earth. We aren't told when the morning stars sang together, and all the sons of God shouted for joy — so that must not be important information for us. We do know the leader of the rebellion and his followers were cast out of Heaven. He couldn't usurp the throne of God so Satan coveted earth. He loathed Adam and Eve — created in God's image. He couldn't rightfully rule earth — but he could steal it if he could get Adam and Eve to commit high treason against God.

His plan worked. Satan became the ruler of this earth for a time — but his days were numbered. At the cross Jesus, the spotless Lamb of God, provided the payment for our sins by His own blood.

> *"For the wages of sin is death,*
> *but the free gift of God is eternal life*
> *in Christ Jesus our Lord."*
> Romans 6:23

Satan was defeated. Mankind could now have freedom from evil — if we wanted it. You memorized this when you were a boy, Josh.

> *"For God so loved the world, that he*
> *gave his one and only Son,*
> *that whoever believes in him should*
> *not perish, but have eternal life."*
> John 3:16

The free gift of salvation has been offered for over 2,000 years — but the time of God's grace is nearly over. You are in the very last days — called the time of Jacob's trouble.

According to Scripture — Israel will sign a seven-year peace treaty with the Antichrist. The God of Abraham, Isaac and Jacob is giving His people, Israel, one final chance to turn to Him. The Jews have a chance to recognize their Messiah — and they will — but sadly, they will follow a false Messiah — the Antichrist — for three and a half years first.

This man of sin will appear with many lying signs and wonders. He will be an amazing orator — a peacemaker — speaking lies to establish a one world terror dictatorship. He will mimic the God of the Universe with his own unholy trinity — the Antichrist, the False Prophet, and the Beast. Ten kings leading ten kingdoms will follow this wicked trio.

This man of sin will stand — filled with demonic power — in the newly built temple in Jerusalem — declaring he is God. Israel will then realize they have been deceived — they have followed a false Messiah. They will flee to a place in the wilderness — many believe it's Petra — where God will care for them for the last three and a half years — for the time called The Great Tribulation.

This will be a time of unprecedented terror for the world. Satan will use the Antichrist to unleash his full fury on the people of earth. It will be the most horrific time the earth has ever seen. If God didn't shorten the days no flesh would be saved (Matthew 24:22).

Countless millions will die for their new faith — the Bible says they will be beheaded. If you choose to follow Christ you will have to fight for your salvation — it won't be as easy as it was in the church age.

> *"Because iniquity will abound, the*
> *love of many will grow cold.*
> *But he who endures to the end will be saved."*
> *Matthew 24:12-13*

You won't be able to buy or sell — unless you have the Mark of the Beast on your forehead or your hand — so you will be totally dependent on God. I trust He will provide for you. If you take the Mark you will be separated from God forever. **DO NOT TAKE THE MARK!!!**

Your Ma and I pray you will be strong and overcome the dark forces of the evil one. The prayers of countless Christians who have gone before you are with you.

God has many witnesses who will bring the gospel to the world. He will raise up 144,000 men from the nation of Israel who will not bow the knee to the Antichrist or become part of his evil kingdom. They will be marked with a seal of the living God on their foreheads, and will go out with the power and anointing of God, to evangelize in all the earth. You will hear of two witnesses in Jerusalem and an angel will fly in the midst of heaven proclaiming the everlasting gospel. If you accept Christ you also will be called to be a witness.

Bibles will most likely be destroyed. You will have to hide yours. All media will be controlled by the government. There is much more. See Matthew 24 for more information.

The awesome news is God wins! At the end of the seven-year time of Jacob's trouble Jesus will return with His bride— God will triumph and the earth will be restored to the way it was in the garden. Satan will be bound for one thousand years. Jesus will rule the nations at that time of global peace called the Millennium. Even animals will live at peace with one-another. It will be glorious.

I pray you'll turn to Christ today before the great deception. Remember, y'all are here on earth because you chose to be. You decided you didn't need God. I hope you realize now you need Him desperately. God has sent you a lifeline. It is this letter.

I pray you will listen — that you realize you are sinners in need of a Savior. Your Ma and I pray you will call upon the Lord while you have a chance. I have studied the Bible since I could read and I believe it is 100% truth. Perilous, savage days are ahead. The odds of y'all surviving the seven years are very slim. To be spared the wrath to come for all eternity in Hell — I suggest you pray this prayer.

"Lord Jesus,

I am sorry I have hardened my heart against You — I refused to believe You are the Messiah. Please forgive me—forgive all my sins. I believe You are the Son of God — that You died on the cross in my place. Thank You that Your blood was shed for me so I could

> *be forgiven. Cleanse me from all unrighteousness. Create in me a clean heart. Please come into my heart, come into my life, fill me with Your Holy Spirit.*
>
> *I realize in my own strength I can do nothing. Thank You I am saved by Your mercy and grace — not because of anything good I have done. Your Name is the only Name in Heaven or on earth by which mankind can be saved. Thank You that my name is written in the Lamb's Book of Life. Please lead me by Your Holy Spirit as I walk earth's perilous final days.*
>
> *Thank You, Lord God."*
>
> John, the beloved disciple — while a prisoner on the island of Patmos — saw a multitude standing in Heaven so great no man could number it. (Revelation 7:9-17). He saw the ones who will be saved out of the Great Tribulation. If you just asked Jesus to be your Savior you will be among that crowd.
>
> I pray God's peace will be with you. You will need His peace to carry you through the dark days ahead. Jesus said,
>
>> *"Peace I leave with you. My peace I give unto you; not as the world gives, I give to you. Don't let your heart be troubled, neither let it be fearful."*
>> *John 14:27*
>
> Your Ma and I love y'all and
> pray we see you again.
> Love, Pa

By the time Josh finished reading Pa's letter they were both in tears. They prayed Pa's prayer together. They knew following Christ on the narrow path would be the hardest road they could possibly choose but it would be the best.

The Children's Prison

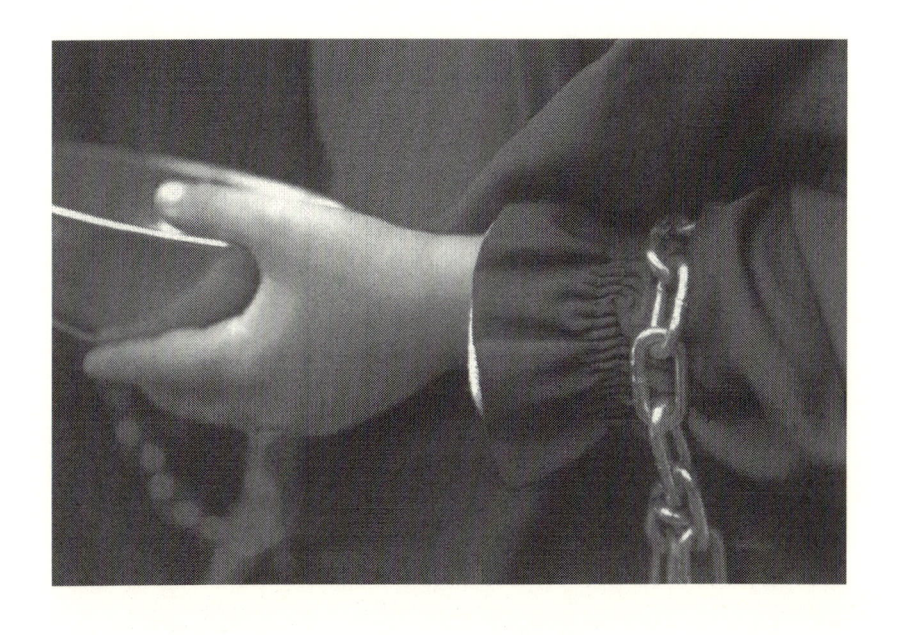

*"Again, therefore, Jesus spoke to them, saying,
"I am the light of the world.
He who follows me will not walk in the darkness,
but will have the light of life."*
John 8:12

MANHUNT

Juliet ducked as another plate was hurled past her head. She wondered why the big man brought her to this scary house. Someone was screaming again. A plate grazed the side of Avely's head. She was eight — a year older than Juliet. Avely ran screaming down the hall and locked herself in the bathroom. Wendy was a year younger. She sobbed from her favorite hiding spot under the table. Juliet hoped she was invisible behind the kitchen door.

Why did these people drink until they acted crazy?
Why were they so mean?
Didn't they know they were scaring their children?
Why wasn't she with Mama and Daddy?
Where were they?
Why didn't they come get her?
Why was she in this scary place?
Her heart was hurting and she wanted to go home.

Finally, it quieted down and the screaming stopped. Things seemed calm. Avely came timidly out of the bathroom. She looked scared. Was there really a truce? Mrs. Zema announced Avely's head was only slightly bruised. There was no blood this time. Nothing to be concerned about.

Maybe the children and the plates would be safe now?

But no, something terrible happened that required immediate justice. Juliet was discovered behind the door and summoned before Mrs. Zema — the presiding judge. Had she opened and eaten some strawberry jam without asking? *How did she know?* All eyes in the courtroom turned to Juliet. How would she plead? She didn't know if confession or a lie would be safer. She chose a lie. A nasty smile spread across the judge's face as she pronounced the verdict. In place of supper there would be a half-teaspoon of dry hot mustard powder.

Mrs. Zema usually resorted to washing all liars' mouths out with soap — this particular liar seemed unrepentant — this was a repeat conviction — the sentencing had to be more drastic. Mrs. Zema measured out the powder into a spoon. Juliet was told it had to stay in her mouth for one minute — the burning seemed to go on forever. She resolved not to steal or lie again. At that moment she hated strawberry jam.

After the mustard powder, Mrs. Zema didn't feel like the little ward of the government was fully repentant. There would have to be further consequences. The guilty party would sleep in the dark, scary, unfinished basement for the night. The only light in the blackness was when the gas furnace randomly bleeped on and there was a glow from the flame.

The little cot and a jam cupboard in the corner were the only furniture in the unfinished basement. Juliet lay there with huge, terrified eyes. She wondered when she would see Mama and Daddy again.

Mr. Zema sat reading the paper as his wife came into the living room. She smiled brightly at him — as if he hadn't recently been the target of her plate throwing. She seemed happy now justice had been done to the naughty girl.

"I don't know how long I can put up with that brat," Mrs. Zema announced to the air. Her husband was engrossed in his newspaper so merely grunted in agreement. That was enough for Mrs. Zema so she continued.

"The little brat has only been here for a week and already I've had to wash her mouth out with soap five times. *Five times!* I had to use dry, hot mustard powder on that wretch tonight. You'd think she'd learn not to steal and lie."

"She seems like such a nice little soul," Mr. Zema muttered under his breath.

"What? Not at all. She's a horrid child. In fact, I'm gonna make sure she goes to prison. Such an incorrigible, hopeless little terror!"

Mr. Zema bravely spoke up. "What're you gonna do?"

"I'm gonna call the agency in the morning and tell them they have to come over an' fetch her. I don't want her pollutin' our little girls with her lyin' thieven' ways. It's prison for her!"

Mr. Zema grunted his disapproval of the plan.

"The children's prison is no place for a seven-year-old. I thought ten-year olds were the youngest sent there."

Mrs. Zema looked so enraged — *how dare he challenge her decision?* He quickly looked away — pretending to be engrossed in the newspaper. He didn't want to create another scene.

Moments later — something in the headlines caught his eye. Mr. Zema sat bolt upright and exclaimed, "Listen to this! It says in this here paper Russia, Iran, and Turkey have joined forces to attack Israel. They say World War III's about to begin."

"Fake news, right?"

"No. This ain't a joke. Iran says they're ready and willing to use their nuclear warheads to wipe Israel off the map. They're saying Israel is 'The Little Satan'. They plan to turn their missiles on 'The Great Satan' — the USA — next. God help us!"

Lying in the darkness, Juliet tried to sort out her thoughts. She had never known terror until someone knocked on the door of her house. She and Mama had been in the kitchen making dinner for Daddy — until that knock her life had been safe — she knew nothing but love and affection. Everything changed with that knock. Why did those mean men come? Why did they want her Daddy?

Had it been only days before Daddy told her stories about when Pa was a little boy from a far-away land? Daddy told her Grandpa was born in a place called the Netherlands. Grandpa's family moved to Alabama when he was a small boy. Josh told her things his Pa told him about Holland — tiny rabbits hopped everywhere — tulips bloomed over huge fields — canals with little bridges seemed to cover all waterways. Dutch cheese was world famous and windmills were strewn across the land. Wooden shoes were everywhere — they were often filled with flowers and sat on people's porches. Many churches had huge pipe organs and massive church bells rang out on Sundays. Bicycles could be seen everywhere. Daddy said Grandpa remembered very little Dutch as it had been replaced by his Southern drawl. He remembered enough to call her "*mijn mooie kleine meisje,* "my beautiful little girl."

The furnace pilot light startled her awake every time it bleeped to life. "*Daddy. Please come find me,*" Juliet whispered into the darkness.

Juliet thought about Mama — her gentle smile, golden hair and kind blue eyes. Juliet desperately wanted Mama to hold her.

"*Mama, where are you?*"

They baked cookies and bread to surprise Daddy. She was Mama's little helper. Her mouth watered as she thought how she would love to have just one cookie. Even a bite of one cookie would be so lovely. She tried not to think about food but it was hard because she was so hungry. She hadn't eaten for days because she had been told she was so naughty.

Juliet thought of her little garden under her bedroom window. She loved looking out and admiring her carrots, cabbages, and peas. Mama grew antique purple, orange and scarlet sunflowers — thankfully a few volunteered to grow in Juliet's garden. They would take flowers, bread and vegetables to sell at the farmer's market. Anything that didn't sell they would take to a seniors' home to give to the elderly. Juliet fell asleep dreaming about brilliantly colored sunflowers and Mama's cookies. She dreamed of tasting sweet little peas.

The furnace bleeped to life. Juliet lay in the darkness — mesmerized by the flames. The room was so black she tried not to look at it. She tried not to think about the jam cupboard by the stairs. She was so hungry she was tempted to steal a jar of delicious jam — but she knew if she did that more horrid things would happen. The darkness seemed to close around her so she decided thinking happy thoughts might help.

MANHUNT

Juliet thought about Mama and Daddy. She knew they loved her so she wondered why they didn't come get her. They also told her they loved God — the most loving Daddy ever — the one who made everything — the sun, the beautiful flowers, Boots, their black horse — everything. They told her He would love her forever and she should trust Him.

The TV was blaring upstairs. Someone was saying world hunger was at epic proportions. What did epic mean? Someone said food was to be rationed further. Did rationed mean less food? She was already so hungry. She heard the TV announcer say several beasts had fatally attacked hundreds of people in the wastelands near the Territories. Somehow the fence had been torn down and several escaped. What did fatally attacked mean? Avely and Wendy told her evil, nasty, hungry beasts lived behind big fences. What was a beast? What were the Territories? Why did the man on TV say such scary things?

"*God,*" she whispered. "*Can You hear me? It's me, Juliet. Do You really love me? Mama and Daddy said You do. Please can I go home?*"

Juliet fell asleep asking God questions.

She dreamed she was flying. She kind of soared over the treetops. It was strange — in her dream, God spoke to her. It wasn't with words she could hear with her ears — it was words she heard with her heart. He told her because people were bad — He had to judge the earth, like in the days of Noah. Mama told her about Noah. The people of earth were so bad God covered the earth with water. Everything was destroyed except a big boat and some people and animals in it. When she looked down from the treetops in her dream — people were dying from swords, hunger, and hungry beasts of the earth. The beasts were like lions and tigers she saw at a zoo — except bigger and scarier.

She wondered why God would show her this. She hadn't said it out loud — only thought her question — God answered in her heart again. He told her He loved her and would keep her safe in the secret place of the Most High — under the shadow of the Almighty. He promised He would hold her close and keep her safe. Juliet settled into a deep, peaceful sleep knowing God was with her.

The next morning the big scary man was back. He looked at Juliet with dark, angry eyes. Juliet wondered why he looked so nasty. Mrs. Zema told the man she was kind of sad to see the little brat go. She winked at the man as she told him she really liked the extra rations. Mrs. Zema laughed at her own joke. The big man said they would try to find her a better-behaved kid so she wouldn't lose the extra rations she deserved for her care of these wayward children.

Avely and Wendy didn't dare look at Juliet as she left or they would have cried. They realized Juliet was a kind girl — she hadn't told Mrs. Zema all three of them ate the strawberry jam.

Juliet was taken to a juvenile detention center. After reading Mrs. Zema's report the Children's Tribunal determined she could not be trusted in any of their foster homes. Who knew what else this lying, thieving little delinquent would do in one of their good homes? She had already been in the best. Juliet was assigned to the children's prison — the youngest child ever sent there. The children's prison had been designed for juvenile delinquents aged ten to eighteen. The Tribunal hoped the prison would knock some sense into this horrid seven-year-old child.

The black van drove deep into the country for about an hour. Juliet was intrigued by an enormous gray building in the middle of a huge field. It was surrounded by a thick, dark forest. She wondered what it could possibly be and was startled when they turned off the highway towards that building. There was high, razor barb-wired fence lining both sides of the road and surrounding the field. Juliet saw girls standing behind that electric fence — staring at her with vacant, empty eyes. The arrival of new wards was the only thing that broke the monotony of their lives.

Juliet had never heard of a children's prison. Once a child was placed within those walls, they remained there, a permanent ward of the government until they were eighteen. Tall watchtowers, manned by people with high-powered rifles, ensured escape was impossible.

Huge iron gates swung open as the driver showed his pass. The building was as cold and gray inside as it was outside. It smelled of bleach — so deathly quiet — their shoes echoed as they walked the long hallway past the jail cells.

The processing room was as cold as the people. Ugly black clothes that looked like pajamas were tossed at her. Someone barked at her to go into a closet and put them on. When she came out, Juliet was shocked to see her clothes being dumped into a garbage can.

The next thing was terrifying — a guard put chains on her wrists. Biting her lip so she wouldn't cry, Juliet wondered if this was a nightmare. Maybe she would wake up soon? The guard, seeing her fear, told her the chain was to keep her safe. Inmates were chained together so while they worked outside the fence they wouldn't get lost.

A woman who looked like she was the boss gave the guard a nasty look. "Prisoners don't need things explained to them!" she barked at the guard.

Juliet found out later this barking woman was named 'Mam' — in charge of the safety and security of the prisoners, the workers, and the prison itself. She didn't stand for any guards showing kindness.

Juliet was escorted to a cell not much bigger than her closet at home. The number crudely painted above the door was 77. Juliet was told she would not be called her name any longer but must answer to 77. The tiny room had a bed, a sink, a toilet and a small dresser. One bare light bulb hung in the middle of the ceiling. Juliet dropped onto the cot in a daze. It was the same kind of cot Mrs. Zema had in the basement. She wondered if the prison also gave naughty girls dry, hot mustard powder.

Some of these children had been traumatized by life. Some had been mentally, physically or sexually abused so were brought here for their 'protection'. In this place, children's souls were shrivelling and dying. Lives were being destroyed as hope for love, beauty or kindness was gone. The mental, emotional, spiritual, and physical wellbeing of the children was neglected. The darkness was so deep Juliet could feel it. It felt even darker than the scary basement. She fell asleep crying.

It seemed like moments later a loud buzzer blared throughout the prison. It was still night. All the prison doors clanged open. Bewildered — not knowing what to do — Juliet lay frozen on the cot. A guard came to her door and screamed, "77! What are you doin' lyin' around? Who do you think you are, a princess? This ain't a palace. Get out here. NOW!"

The guard came into the cell and grabbed Juliet by her arm as she apparently hadn't moved fast enough. She was dragged to the door and commanded to stand there for inspection. Juliet heard a bird outside the high, barred window. At least he's free, she thought. A row of guards and robots slowly made their way down the hallway. Juliet had never seen an AI before. They looked almost human, but something was missing. An AI came up to Juliet and touched her hair.

"This one's got lice."

A guard grabbed and half dragged her down the long hallway to the infirmary. Juliet knew she didn't have lice. A friend once had lice. They were little bugs that bit your head and made it itchy. Her head wasn't itchy. Why were the guards so mean to her? Did Mrs. Zema tell them she was a really bad girl? Is that why they were so nasty?

The infirmary was a cold, sterile room full of steel tubs for baths. Juliet shivered as she sat in one of the tubs. Something was poured over her head — her skin burned but she didn't dare say anything. The guards forgot about her while they visited. Just as she thought she couldn't stand the burning any longer buckets of cold water were poured over her head. She was dragged back to her cell dripping wet and cold. Even though it was summer the warmth didn't penetrate the walls of that place.

Days were spent picking rocks in a large quarry. It seemed the goal was to move rocks from one pile to another and then back to the first pile — exhausting, pointless work. The inmates liked mocking her and calling her a baby because she couldn't lift heavy rocks. Juliet tried to be brave during the day and cried into her pillow at night.

One evening, Juliet was surprised to find a very small Bible in the back of her little dresser drawer. She hadn't seen it there before. Had one of the workers placed it there? That seemed impossible. She hadn't met a kind person in the prison — except the guard the first day — but hadn't seen her again. Bibles were forbidden —she wasn't sure why it hadn't been discovered. Sneaking it to her little cot she hid it under her pillow.

Juliet read the precious word of God every night when everyone was sleeping. She was thankful the lights were left on all night. Cameras on the walls allowed the guards to watch her but if she pulled the thin sheet over her head she couldn't be seen. Thankfully the sheet was so thin light shone through.

She thought about a sign she had once seen,

> *"I believe in the sun even when it isn't shining.*
> *I believe in love, even when I can't feel it.*
> *I believe in God, even when He is silent."*

It was a message she had seen in a book — a message written on a cellar wall during the Holocaust. She wondered what a Holocaust was. Was that happening in the world now? Juliet whispered into her pillow,

"I trust you, God. I do believe in the sun even when I can't see it. I believe in love even when I can't feel it. And I believe in You, God, even when You are silent."

Juliet read in her Bible,

> *"Again, therefore, Jesus spoke to them, saying,*
> *"I am the light of the world.*
> *He who follows me will not walk in darkness,*
> *but will have the light of life."*
> *John 8:12*

Juliet whispered into her pillow, "*Dear God, please may I not walk in darkness. Please may I have Your light of life. Please, God, keep my Mama and Daddy safe. Please could You help them find me?*"

PART 3

SHEEP AMONG WOLVES

Sheep Among Wolves

*"For I know that after my departure,
vicious wolves will enter in among you,
not sparing the flock.
Men will arise from among your own selves,
speaking perverse things,
to draw away the disciples after them."
Acts 20:29-30*

MANHUNT

Lying in Tom's hayloft, Josh watched a little bat use his sonar to locate bugs. What an amazing thing. Tormenting thoughts of being discovered made all other distracting thoughts welcome. Josh's thoughts drifted back to the Rapture. Was it really three years ago? It seemed like a lifetime ago. They had been back in the U.S. for about four years when the disappearance happened. Ma and Pa tried to warn them it was imminent but they didn't pay attention. They thought Ma and Pa were religious fanatics so they didn't take much stock in what they said.

Ma told little Juliet about Jesus until Josh asked her to stop. He felt religion was something Juliet could choose later if she wanted. He didn't want her brainwashed or pressured into something — now he wished she had been given the opportunity to accept Jesus as her Savior.

Why were we so stupid?
What were we thinking?
Why hadn't we listened?

After the disappearance everything changed. Josh and Rachel realized too late their parents had told them the truth. They wished they had accepted Christ before the Rapture — but it was too late for regrets.

Desperate to learn more about God, Josh took Bible classes once a week — in secret — at a friend's home. Bibles were being confiscated and burned so had to be hidden. Pa left a library with lots of books about end times. His Bible was full of notes in the margins explaining things. He wrote a 'Mark of the Beast' would be implemented at the half-way point — three and a half years into the Tribulation. Those who refused the mark would be beheaded. Josh had to warn others. They were only months away from that timeline.

Josh realized before the Rapture many had been deceived — the same deception still blinded many people's eyes. Many had a head knowledge of God but no heart understanding. He realized people had listened to false teachers — wolves — who said the Bible wasn't really God's inspired Word. It was just a bunch of interesting stories.

False churches, false pastors, false prophets and false evangelists abounded before and after the Rapture. Many who thought they were Christians before the disappearance realized too late they were not. They had a head knowledge of God but had not given their lives to Him. They had religion and not a relationship with Christ. They were left behind.

The time was short and Josh realized this was his last chance to tell others to flee from the wrath to come. Many professing Christians abandoned the narrow path and flirted with things of darkness. Some believed the lie — Bible prophesy was not for today — too controversial and must be avoided. It was thought people would be scared away with talk about Jesus' return and coming judgement. Many didn't want to be disturbed by hearing about Hell.

The king's Prophet — revered by the masses — taught there are many paths to God — that there is unity among all religions. Many followed false teachers. Folks couldn't see they were following wolves. Part of the problem was sometimes you couldn't tell the wolves from the sheep. They looked identical. The only way you knew for sure you were dealing with a wolf was by their fruit. Wolves left a wake of destruction.

> *"Beware of false prophets, who come*
> *to you in sheep's clothing,*
> *but inwardly are ravening wolves.*
> *By their fruits you will know them.*
> *Do you gather grapes from thorns or figs from thistles?"*
> *Matthew 7:15-16*

Many said science was superior to God. Who did they think created science? Some claimed man evolved from nothing — lifeless sub-atomic particles just came together and created the complexities of life. Scientifically impossible. Insanity.

MANHUNT

It became clear to Josh, when man refuses to honor God, he becomes morally bankrupt — led by the flesh instead of the Spirit of God. Josh pleaded with people to listen to the Word of God — his pleas often fell on deaf ears. Many chose to turn their backs on truth and listened to fables.

Many church leaders who were left behind after the Rapture preached a social gospel — helping the poor — the homeless — banning nuclear weapons — saving the environment — reducing poverty. These are important things, but there's a problem. People were being helped for this life but there was no concern for their eternal destiny.

Josh helped serve at a soup kitchen hoping to tell people about Christ, but was told 'witnessing' wasn't allowed. He handed out sandwiches to homeless people, but was not allowed to give out the words of eternal life — to tell them about Heaven or Hell. People's stomachs were being filled while their souls were starving. The social gospel left the church vulnerable to wolves.

In order to appear up-to-date and to comply with the Prophet's global church, in keeping with the times, many churches before and after the disappearance embraced things that break God's heart. Church leaders blessed abortion clinics, same sex-marriages, and the ordination of homosexuals as church leaders (they mustn't have read Romans 1).

There was apostasy and deception — the love of many grew cold. Many had a low tolerance for conflict and didn't want to make waves by standing for truth. They didn't want to be rejected. They didn't seem to realize, by stepping off the narrow path, they were choosing the swift descent onto the wide road of destruction.

Many loved the praise of men more than the praise of God. Jesus said they hated Me so they will hate you. People were afraid of being hated. They chose to be silent. Churches were "seeker sensitive" and refused to speak of the fearsome realities of sin and Hell. They refused to warn people that one day a Holy God would pour out His wrath on an unrepentant world.

Josh realized — too late — when God's gospel of grace is trivialized people don't see the need to repent. He hadn't seen his own need to get right with God before the disappearance. People didn't realize they were in a war and were being taken hostage by evil. They were becoming the prey of terrible *"principalities, powers, rulers of the darkness of this world, and spiritual wickedness in high places"*. (Ephesians 6:12)

A year after the Rapture, just before all churches closed, Josh and Rachel visited a missionary training centre. They were shocked at the 'moral government' heresy being taught. Students were told God doesn't know everything — the sacrifice of Jesus was not necessary. Josh said that was blasphemy. Without the shed blood of Jesus there is no forgiveness for sin.

People seemed to blindly believe whatever they were told. Rachel asked one of the teachers if the Book of Revelation was an actuality or a possibility. He said it was a possibility. Rachel heard God's voice thundering inside her,

"HEAVEN AND EARTH WILL PASS AWAY, BUT MY WORD WILL BY NO MEANS PASS AWAY!"
Luke 21:33

According to the logic of the school's teachers — the future was unknown — even to God. Josh thought the teachers were delusional — the blind were leading the blind. He saw the growing apostasy and tried to warn people they were being deceived. He told folks it was wise to be discerning and ask questions.

"But the Spirit says expressly that in later times some will fall away from the faith, paying attention to seducing spirits and doctrines of demons..."
I Timothy 4:1

Josh heard of a missionary who taught the Bible is just fables. He told people a loving God would not send millions to Hell because they didn't believe in Jesus. He said they could accept Christ after they died — that when they met Him they could choose to accept or reject Him then. This missionary was preaching another gospel — creating a god he could live with but not the true God revealed in the Bible. Because he did not believe in Hell, even though Jesus talked about it more than Heaven, he chose to deny its existence. Jesus warned folks to flee from the wrath to come. Josh told people trusting in these lies was sending people into a godless eternity.

> "...As he sat on the Mount of Olives, the disciples came to him privately, saying, "Tell us, when will these things be? What is the sign of your coming, and of the end of the age?" Jesus answered them, "Be careful that no one leads you astray."
> Matthew 24:3-4

The first sign of Jesus' return is deception.

Josh thought it should be obvious to any thinking person that God's mercy only lasts so long before judgement falls. That's what happened after the Rapture. Those who were salt and light had been removed from every nation. The chaos that followed was unimaginable. It was a horrible time for those who chose to reject God.

For those who afterwards chose God, there was a brief moment in time to tell others eternal truths. Josh wondered if any he tried to warn reported his rebellious attitudes to the Grand Tribunal. Was that what made him a target of the Manhunters?

Love Not Your Life Unto Death

*"They overcame him because of the Lamb's blood,
and because of the word of their testimony.
They didn't love their life, even to death."
Revelation 12:11*

MANHUNT

Rachel shivered as she woke up under a thin sheet. A single light hung from a chord above her head. She surveyed the small room — so dark it was impossible to tell if it was night or day. There had been windows but they were boarded up. There was a small table near the wall covered in surgical instruments.

What was this? A hospital? It looked like a hospital room — except very old and grimy.

Her head was throbbing. Had someone hit her? Why did they bring her here?

Rachel heard footsteps outside the door so she pretended to be asleep. Voices murmured. As the door burst open a gruff male voice demanded, "How can she still be sleeping? Did you give her too much chloroform?"

"We could wake her up," suggested a whiny voice.

"Nah. It's okay. We have time."

Rachel wondered, *"Time for what?"*

She heard the door close and sounds of footsteps echoing down a hall.

Rachel's last memories before waking up were of a huge man yelling at her to tell them where Josh was. She had no idea.

Why did they want her husband? Who were these people? Why had they been in her house? It was all so confusing.

Juliet had been crying so she had reached out to comfort her daughter. That's when someone grabbed Juliet and hauled her to a van.

Rachel screamed, "Don't take my baby girl!"

Everything went black. She'd been drugged. Her body felt like ice and her stomach demanded food. Even though she just woke up she felt like sleeping again. Was she still being drugged?

Closing her eyes for what seemed like a moment Rachel fell into a deep sleep. Her dream was so serene. She was walking in her garden with Juliet — there was an abundance of sunflowers. All was tranquil until a dark cloud overshadowed the scene.

—∽—

Rachel woke with a start. How long had she slept? Where was she? Where was her husband? Her little girl?

She could hear voices in the hall.

"How do we know she's one of them? Maybe it's a mistake?" a voice whined.

"Nah. She's one of them alright. Didn't ya see the little cross she was wearin'?"

"Maybe somebody gave it to her and she doesn't know nuthin."

"Naw. We got us here an enemy of the state and we're gonna make her turn away from the lies she's believin'."

"What if she won't change her mind?"

"Ha! If she don't — well — the state has ways of makin' people change how they think."

Rachel felt chilled as she heard hideous laughter.

"Ya hear me? Those Christians are enemies of the state. We are doin' the king a favor when we get rid of 'em. Them's vermin — that's all they is. They ain't helpin' us at all."

"Why do ya say that?"

"They resist our worshipin' Lord Maitreya, our king. They are stoppin' our evolvin' to the next level. The king said so."

"All hail the king. The king is wise," the whiny voice snivelled.

"Yup. He's gonna' save the world. He told us so."

"How's he gonna do that?"

"Well…he's dealin' with them Christians. They's the ones who won't come 'round to our way of thinkin'."

"Why did the aliens leave Christians behind then?" the whiny voice wondered aloud.

"They didn't leave them. Many became Christians after the disappearance. Stupid, ignorant people."

The whiny voice asked, "Why didn't they send her to the Territories? Ain't that what they normally do with her kind?"

"Nah. Probably the guillotine."

"So, why did they bring her to this re-education center?"

"They need her. She knows where her husband is. If we can find out we are gonna' get a huge reward. For some reason he's important to Lord Maitreya."

There was a loud, clattering sound in the hallway. The voices got louder.

"You're such a stupid imbecile! Can't ya' do anything right," a mean voice yelled.

"I'm sorry," a small voice snivelled.

"All the needles for our patients are broken. Can't you carry a tray without trippin? Now we have to get more needles — it could take days. You're such a stupid fool!"

There were scuffling sounds — a voice cried out. There was a thud like someone falling — then it got very quiet.

Rachel was at a re-education center? She didn't want to face that reality. She allowed her mind to wander to thoughts of her deployment with the Marines in Afghanistan. The people in the Hindu Kush mountains had been assured they would be kept safe by the occupying forces. Without warning the Brotherhood — the Marines who had been deployed to guard the people — were called home.

There were hopes the rebel forces coming in would not harm the civilians. Was that wishful thinking? After their departure Rachel learned Christians were driven from their homes and their ancestral lands if they refused to bow their knees to Allah. Rachel wondered what happened to them. Had they felt what she was feeling now? She felt stressed — disconnected — she knew from her doctoral training she had to be strong to survive — but she didn't have the strength to face the dangers of the re-education center alone.

"Dear God, please help me be courageous. Help me be strong for You — no matter what happens to never deny You. Protect my family, please. Thank You, Lord."

Rachel thought about many around the world who loved not their lives unto death. Many faced imprisonment, torture and death rather than deny Christ. Jim Elliot once said. *"He is no fool who gives what he cannot keep to gain what he cannot lose."* He was a missionary to the Waodani, a tribe of fierce warriors in Ecuador, South America — martyred by the ones he had gone to serve. After his murder, his wife Elizabeth and their young daughter went to live among the Waodani. Elizabeth wanted to show these precious people the love and forgiveness of God.

Rachel wanted to be like those brave people. She whispered a verse to comfort her heart, *"When I am afraid, I will trust in You."*

Now it was her turn to decide. Would she be faithful unto death if that was required? *"God, please give me strength."*

The door banged open and a nurse appeared wheeling a cart holding several bowls of cold, lumpy looking porridge.

The nurse pulled up a chair and watched Rachel eat the slimy meal. He was talkative. Rachel was thankful because he was her source of information.

He told Rachel it was a sunny day outside. So — it was day. He quickly switched topics and informed her shock therapy reprogrammed people's minds.

The nurse smiled broadly as he informed her, "The doctors talk a lot about neuroplasticity. They say that's how the brain forms neural connections and new thoughts. This often happens after an injury or trauma. We provide both."

"What do you mean?"

The nurse continued smiling as he announced, "We use a very small element of torture to help people think properly. It works well. We give people new thoughts."

The nurse seemed happy to have a willing listener.

"A human behavior specialist named Dr. Demartini used techniques to restructure the brain. We learned from the best. If someone doesn't respond well to the 'treatments' then we have to perform a frontal lobotomy. That's a kind of neurosurgery — severs the brain itself from the prefrontal cortex. People become very childlike and obedient to our teachings — loyal supporters of the king. So wonderful."

The nurse suddenly stopped speaking. As if in a trance he stood at attention, gave a Nazi salute, and robotically declared, "Hail Messiah! Long live the king!" He then marched out of the room. Rachel wondered if the nurse had a frontal lobotomy or was somehow connected to a computer that reprogrammed his brain. She could hear marching steps all the way down the hall.

The trolley with bowls of porridge still sat in the corner. Rachel was sad for the people who were hungrily waiting for their horrid food. A rat scurried towards the bowls. She whispered, *"Lord God, I commit my life into Your hands."*

Rachel tried to get up but was strapped to the cot. *"Lord, I am so cold with just this thin sheet. Please could I be warm?"* Rachel suddenly felt like she was being held — surrounded by the love of God. It felt like a warm blanket.

"Thank You, Lord, I am held by Your peace that passes all understanding.

Thank You, greater are You who is in me than He who is in the world.

Thank You, I have not been given a spirit of fear, but of power, love and a sound mind.

You alone have the words of eternal life. I trust You, Lord.

Thank You, one day — maybe soon — the trials of this life will be over.

One day there will be no more tears, no more pain, no more evil, no more babies being slaughtered, no more children being abused, no more racial conflicts, no more religious persecution, no more selling of people's bodies and souls, no more depravity and man's evil hearts.

One day those who love You will be like You— and it will be more beautiful and amazing than we could ever imagine.

Thank You, that You called me out of darkness and invited me to be part of Your eternal family.

I am forever grateful.

I love You, Lord God. My Abba."

Rachel fell asleep feeling enveloped by the love of God.

Released

*"Be strong and courageous.
Don't be afraid or scared of them;
for Yahweh your God himself is who goes with you.
He will not fail you nor forsake you."*
Deuteronomy 31:6

Rachel dreamed of a story she once heard from World War II. It happened in May, 1940. Germany invaded the Netherlands. The Nazis were hunting Jews. Caspar Ten Boom opened his home in Haarlem to protect God's chosen people — creating a hiding place for his Jewish guests. The Ten Booms were part of a group called the *Dutch Underground* or *Resistance*.

In the dream, Rachel saw a banner that said 1944. She saw a Dutch informer notify the Germans of the hidden Jews. Perhaps he felt it would give him a chance to live? Maybe he traded people's lives for cigarettes and ration cards. Whatever his motive — Rachel watched as the Ten Booms and thirty-five others were arrested. She saw several eventually sentenced to Nazi concentration death camps.

In her dream, Rachel watched Corrie Ten Boom being imprisoned and kept in solitary confinement for three months in Holland. One day Corrie was interrogated by a Nazi lieutenant. Rachel watched as Corrie told him of her work with mentally disabled people. The lieutenant laughed at how ludicrous it was to help someone with a disability. Corrie courageously defended her work and asserted in God's eyes a mentally disabled person might be more valuable than a watchmaker, like her father, or even a lieutenant.

She was sent to the notorious Ravensbruck concentration camp in Germany. Months later, Corrie was summoned to stand in front of a clerk. She assumed it was to be given her death sentence. Rachel rejoiced as she watched Corrie being told she was free to leave — she just had to agree to sign a paper saying she had been treated humanely at the camp. Corrie found out later the release was because of a clerical error. The following week all women in her age group were executed.

Rachel awoke thinking about the dream. It had been so vivid — as if she had really been there. Why did God give her that dream? She thought about the providence of God that spared Corrie's life. Would God spare her life?

Thoughts of the Holocaust led Rachel to think about the miracle of a nation being born in a day. May 14, 1948 — the fulfilment of an ancient prophesy.

> *"Who has heard of such a thing?*
> *Who has seen such things?*
> *Shall a land be born in one day?*
> *Shall a nation be born at once?*
> *For as soon as Zion travailed,*
> *she gave birth to her children."*
> *Isaiah 66:8*

Rachel considered God's promise to Abraham, *"I will bless those who bless you and curse those who curse you; and in you all the families of the earth will be blessed."* It was an irrevocable promise. The Jewish nation gave earth the Bible — the Ten Commandments — Jesus the Messiah — Christianity. Her ancestors were ordained by God to bless the nations by displaying God's wisdom, mercy, salvation, beauty, truth, strength, and healing. It was incredible — mind boggling actually — that such a tiny nation could make such a huge impact on the world.

God promised Abraham the land of Israel would belong to his descendants as an everlasting covenant. Rachel reflected on the miracle of the 1967 six-day war — dramatic proof of God's protection of Israel. This tiny nation was surrounded by multiplied millions of enemies. Although vastly outnumbered — when the smoke cleared in six days — Israel emerged victorious. It was a miracle. No one in their right mind could question that.

Rachel thought about how the prophet Ezekiel once saw a valley of dry bones. Was this a picture of the Jews returning physically to the land but dead spiritually — living far from God? Or was it a picture of them scattered over the earth? God asked Ezekiel if those bones could live. Ezekiel wisely answered, *"O Sovereign LORD, You alone know."* Only God can bring life from death. This was God's amazing reply.

MANHUNT

"Again he said to me,
"Prophesy over these bones, and tell them,
'You dry bones, hear Yahweh's word.
The Lord Yahweh says to these bones:
"Behold, I will cause breath to enter
into you, and you will live.
I will lay sinews on you, and will bring up flesh on you,
and cover you with skin, and put breath
in you, and you will live.
Then you will know that I am Yahweh.'"
Ezekiel 37:4

Rachel knew the bones were modern-day Israel. When God breathed on the lifeless corpses they came to life. Israel would one day come alive spiritually — when the Jewish people recognized Jesus as the Messiah. Sadly, Israel now followed a false Messiah promising a false peace. But that time of deception was almost over.

Many claimed God was finished with Israel.

"Impossible," Rachel whispered. *"Never."*

Many said the nation of Israel today was not really Biblical Israel — that the promises of God to Abraham no longer belonged to his descendants — that the blessings now belonged to Christians. Jews were welcome to keep the curses.

"So stupid — by belittling Israel, folks are destroying the root of the olive tree they're grafted into. Many claim Israel is illegally occupying land You promised them — that it now belongs to the Palestinians. LORD, You see what a deception this is. There <u>never</u> was a nation of Arabs called Palestinians. You promised the land to the Jews as an everlasting Covenant. Thank You for Your faithfulness to my people. How amazing folks today can witness the prophetic fulfilment of the building of the third temple. What a miracle!"

A nurse banged the door open and rolled a wheelchair into the room. The rat abandoned his porridge feast and scurried away. It was the same nurse — the crazy one who appeared to have had a frontal lobotomy.

"Good afternoon."

So, it was afternoon.

"Where am I?"

"You're at Ravensbruck Re-Education Hospital."

Rachel was startled. Ravensbruck was the name of the concentration camp Corrie Ten Boom had been taken to. *Was the dream about Corrie from You, God?*

"This facility was named after a famous concentration camp in World War II. We are using many of their same wonderful techniques here."

The nurse laughed, obviously thinking he was enormously funny. Rachel did not get the joke.

"This isn't just any re-education center. Ravensbruck is famous for its innovations. Have you heard of eugenics?"

Ignoring Rachel's horrified expression, the nurse continued.

"Eugenics, dear, is how we get rid of undesirables — useless eaters — those who don't fit into our dream of a perfect society."

Rachel thought in a perfect society this nurse wouldn't have a chance.

"There is a huge gene selection program going on here at Ravensbruck. There is also a great nano-technology department dedicated to rewriting the genetic codes to create a transhuman, genetically modified race. We are hoping to raise an army of super-soldiers. Oops...I think I've said too much."

"Why am I here then?"

Laughing at Rachel's bewilderment he announced, "It's also a rehabilitation center for folks like you."

"What do they plan to do with me?"

"Your question is perfectly timed. You're about to find out, my dear. The medical team have been eagerly waiting to meet you." He seemed very excited about this meeting.

Rachel thought it sounded ominous.

The nurse smiled broadly at Rachel as if she should be pleased by this news. She ignored the smile. The nurse rolled the wheelchair over to the cot.

MANHUNT

"It's electro-therapy day!" the nurse announced with enthusiasm. "Your vacation has been long enough. Today we begin your re-education. Time to rise and shine!"

She hadn't walked for days — or was it weeks? All sense of time was gone.

"Okay, my dear. We're going for a nice little ride," the nurse gleefully announced.

This was Rachel's first time out of the room. It *was* a hospital — or at least it had been. It was very old and dilapidated. Windows were broken and tiles were lifting off the floor. It looked like it had been through a war.

They passed rooms filled with patients and stopped in front of what appeared to have been an operating room. Several people in white lab coats were waiting for her.

"Now, this surgical suite is where we help folks have politically correct thoughts. Electro-magnetic frequencies will reprogram your brain," someone announced. "Please hop up on this table, my dear."

Rachel thought of fighting — but was too weak from the drugs and lack of food. She thought of trying to run — but realized that wasn't an option — she could barely stand and she had no idea where she could run to. She had no choice but to let the nurse and the people in white help her onto the steel table. Thankfully they gave her a thin sheet.

"Now don't be afraid. This won't hurt a bit," the nurse lied. Electrodes were attached to Rachel's head so electric currents could pass through her brain. She was hooked up to an IV with crystalloid fluid being transfused into her. A heart monitor was hooked up showing when the voltage was too high and there was a danger of a heart attack.

Someone who seemed to be a doctor said, "Hopefully this triggers a seizure. I LOVE electroconvulsive therapy! It gives me such a charge." The doctor laughed at his own joke. Others looked bored. They had heard this joke so many times they were ready to scream.

The doctor continued. "When your brain chemistry has changed, you'll think politically correct thoughts, my dear. Isn't that wonderful?"

Rachel closed her eyes. She had to think of beautiful things to survive this horror. She thought of Josh. Where was he? Was he okay? What was happening with Juliet?

"Dear Abba, thank You for my precious family. Please keep them in Your care. Thank You that You are with me — You will never leave me or forsake me. Ever. Please may these people see Your power. Don't let them take control of my mind. Thank You." She drifted off into a peaceful sleep.

Hours later the doctor announced, "She's ready — lessons in allegiance to the king will begin immediately. Take her to the re-education suite."

The medical team was stymied. They had tried everything in their arsenal to reprogram Rachel's brain but she didn't respond to their best efforts. They just could not take control of her mind. She was the most perplexing patient they ever had. She fiercely clung to her politically incorrect beliefs about God. They had no idea what to do with her. Perhaps a frontal lobotomy was the next option?

The Tribunal was notified. They would advise the doctors how to proceed.

The nurse informed Rachel she was ordered to appear before the Tribunal the next day. Rachel prayed, *"God, please help me."*

After her bowl of bitter tasting porridge, Rachel fell into a deep, drugged sleep.

She dreamed she was flying. It was her strangest dream ever. She was wrapped in a scratchy blanket — flying in a military helicopter. The flight seemed to take hours. Each time she woke someone gave her another sedative.

MANHUNT

The helicopter landed at night by the edge of a deep forest. Blinding lights blazed around the landing pad. Rachel was commanded to follow a soldier along a narrow path. Soldiers with rifles and strobe lights lined the path. She followed the soldier through the forest — then through a door-way that led into the side of a mountain. Rachel followed the soldier down a path that wove through a winding tunnel. Why was she dreaming of a military fortress? Such a strange dream.

Suddenly, the path opened into a dazzlingly bright cave deep in the belly of the mountain. Rachel was astonished to see a garden enclosed by a gigantic glass pyramid. *How could such beauty exist in the depths of a mountain? Where did the light come from for the garden?*

Powerful full spectrum lights illuminated the pyramid. Light refracted from many panes of glass like a billion sparkling diamonds. A skylight bored through the top of the mountain and seemed to touch the sky. The stars twinkled above the pyramid. During the day the garden would be filled with natural light. Everything was breathtakingly beautiful. Rachel wondered if Eden had looked anything like this garden.

The soldier escort disappeared. Rachel was surprised to be left alone. She walked slowly — touching everything — it all felt so real. What an amazing dream! Exotic flowers, shrubs and trees abounded. Brilliant stands of purple irises and fuchsia peonies surrounded a pond of sparkling clear water.

Colorful birds chattered among the trees. An enormous effervescent blue morpho butterfly flitted past Rachel's head. The air was heavy with the scent of sweet orange blossoms. Walking amongst the flowers — the fruit trees — breathing in their fragrances — Rachel stopped to admire the brightly colored fish in a pond.

That's when she heard voices. She vaguely overheard a transaction being made — Josh's life for hers.

This was an extremely strange dream.

She heard someone read a message aloud.

*"By the direct will and order of His Majesty the King -
The Great, Benevolent, Kind and Gracious One -
Dr. Rachel Williams has been pardoned
by the Grand Tribunal."*

A voice said the letter was stamped and sealed with the Great Seal of the Republic by the king himself.

"It's your choice," a voice said. "Does Captain Fred Markert take this letter to the Tribunal at the re-education hospital tomorrow — or does Rachel face the guillotine or the beasts?"

Someone screamed "No!"

The voice sounded so much like Josh's. Rachel heard anguish — deep pain — in that one word. Looking up from the pond — she turned towards the voice. It was Josh!

"My love," she murmured. She smiled at him as their eyes met. There was such a depth of love in those eyes. Moving towards him ever so slowly — Rachel felt like she was sleepwalking — walking under water. The waves held her back — pulling her into darkness. Rachel awoke on the steel table.

Five men in gray military fatigues sat behind an enormous mahogany table. The table and a few chairs were the only furniture in the massive room.

The doctors and nurses stood at attention beside the table. They were apprehensive as they realized their lack of success with Rachel left them open to discipline.

Rachel swooned as she stood before them.

She hadn't walked and had barely eaten since a lifetime ago. They offered her a hard, metal chair.

Rachel had never felt so exhausted in all her life.

She was so thirsty. So hungry.

Rachel realized, with shame, her hair hadn't been washed or combed since she had arrived — her clothes were soiled. She had no idea how long she'd been in the same clothes.

MANHUNT

The Tribunal looked at her with contempt.

They didn't appear to even want to be in the same room with her.

Some held their noses commenting on the stench.

She looked at the floor and slumped down in the chair — trying to give them less of her to be scornful of.

"So, we understand you're a Christian."

Rachel immediately thought of the verse,

"Everyone therefore who confesses me before men,
I will also confess him before my Father who is in Heaven.
But whoever denies me before men,
I will also deny him before my Father who is in Heaven."
Matthew 10:32-33

"Yes," she replied.

She was startled to hear her own voice. It sounded so tired.

A burly man cleared his throat. "Do you know why you're here?" he asked gruffly.

Rachel recognized him. He was the one who put a cloth over her face at her house before everything went black.

"Yes."

Ignoring her reply the man continued, "You're at the best re-education facility in the quadrant. By the time people leave here they are model citizens. And if not..." He grinned at Rachel implying he wanted her to fill in the rest of the sentence.

"Have you information on the whereabouts of your husband?" another voice from the Tribunal demanded.

"No."

Another voice commanded, "Speak up! We can't hear you!"

"I don't know where he is."

Another voice yelled, "Liar! You must know his whereabouts!"

"The polygraph tests determined she really doesn't know," one brave doctor said.

The burly man snarled at the doctor, "You were not asked to speak."

The doctor sheepishly apologized.

The Tribunal Chief faced Rachel and said, "Your behavior has been deemed unacceptable. You were seen by satellite surveillance and facial recognition, taking food to Widow Jennings. She had been assigned death by starvation. There was no permission given for anyone to bring her food. What do you have to say for yourself?"

"Widow Jennings is my friend, Sir. She needed help so I visited her and brought her food. I would do the same for you."

Several on the Tribunal cleared their throats and looked uncomfortable. This was not going as planned. They hoped for a way to frame her for illegal Christian activities.

Rachel had been at the hospital for over a month. She had not responded favorably to any of the treatments. The Tribunal determined she was ineligible for re-education. They decided a frontal lobodomy would be a waste of time. They had no further need of her — so her life had to be terminated. They had a noisy debate among themselves. Would she be sentenced to the guillotine or banished to the Territories?

They came to an agreement. Rachel overheard the word Territories being whispered. Just as the Tribunal was about to pronounce the sentence there was a loud banging on the door.

"Come in!" yelled the burly man.

A small man, dressed in military fatigues, came to attention in the doorway. He saluted as he surveyed the room. He seemed unsure about what to do with himself or the message he carried.

"I said come in!" the burly man hollered again.

The little man apologized and stepped briskly into the room.

"Captain Markert — with a dispatch from the Grand Tribunal. They have decreed the woman, Dr. Rachel Williams, is to be freed."

The Tribunal looked shocked — then horrified at the news.

The burly man asked to see the dispatch. His face went pale — there was no denying the Great Dragon Seal of the Kingdom. He read the pardon aloud.

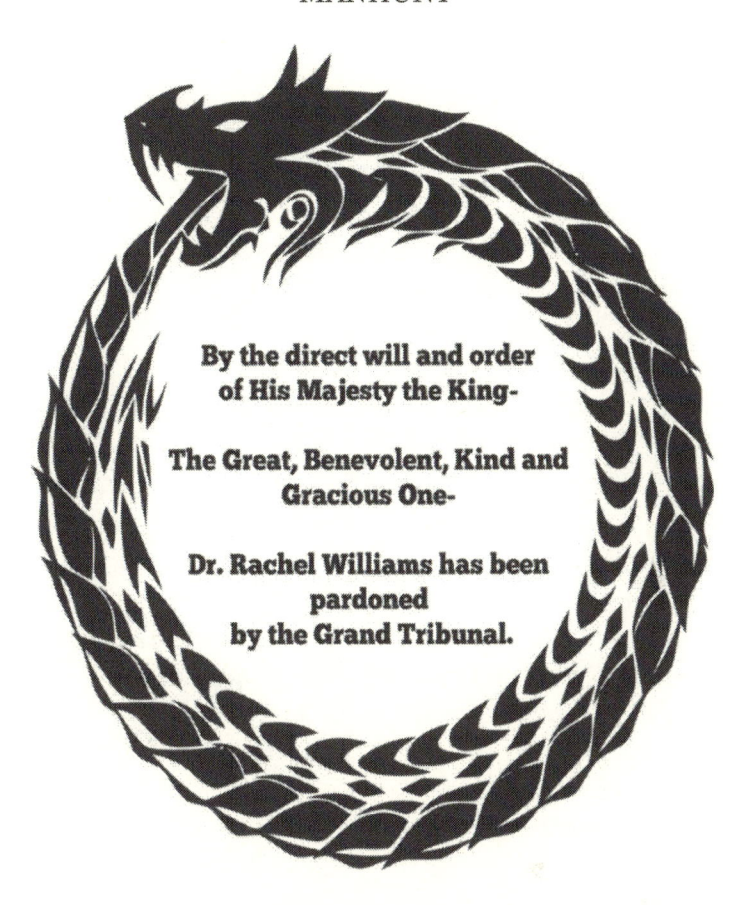

> **By the direct will and order of His Majesty the King—**
>
> **The Great, Benevolent, Kind and Gracious One—**
>
> **Dr. Rachel Williams has been pardoned by the Grand Tribunal.**

Rachel was startled. It seemed she had heard that pardon before — but where? Wasn't that what she heard in her dream? How could that be?

They had no choice but to order the woman to leave — at once — before they were charged with illegally holding a pardoned prisoner and sentenced to death themselves.

Rachel was escorted to a sterile looking room. She hoped she wasn't dreaming again as she lowered her body into a tub of warm, sudsy water. The soap and shampoo were an almost forgotten luxury. Was it really just over a month since she had a bath? Being clean never felt so good.

"Thank You, God, for everything," she whispered.

Rachel was given stale bread — devoured in moments — and asked to sign a document saying she had been treated humanely at the hospital. It would be a lie to sign, however, she had been treated humanely in the last hour. That was her loophole so she wasn't lying.

Rachel wondered if Corrie Ten Boom felt like she was in a dream as the gates of Ravensbruck closed behind her. She could relate. Had God given her the dream of Corrie being freed to prepare her?

As Captain Markert escorted her to the hospital entrance he announced he had been commanded by the Grand Tribunal to give her a ride to her home.

As they got settled in the car, Captain Markert said, "Rachel, your home is a five-hour drive — so just go ahead and rest. I'm sure you must be tired. Oh—you can call me Fred".

"Why don't you talk with a Southern drawl like everyone else around here, Fred?"

"I'm not from around here. My home's in Chicago."

"Why are you so far South?"

"That's classified information."

She thanked Fred for his kindness as she slumped into the car seat and quickly fell into a deep sleep. The weeks of drugs, shock therapy, starvation, sleep deprivation, and emotional stress had been mentally, spiritually, and physically exhausting.

An hour later Fred halted the car at a check-stop. He had to show the soldiers his transit papers. There were tanks lining the road with their turrets pointed at the vehicle. Any suspicious movements and a vehicle would be blasted into oblivion. The guards were posted six feet apart in front of the high wire electric fence for miles. Enormous rolls of razor wire were looped across the top and stretched as far as the eye could see. This was the fence between 'Occupied Land' and 'The Territories'.

Rachel awoke — startled to see a rifle pointed at her head. She was shocked to hear the hungry roaring of the beasts. A guard asked the driver if she was being delivered to the Territories.

Rachel's heart froze. Had she been lied to? Was she really going to be set free or was she being sent to the beasts?

Noticing her fear, Fred quickly calmed her by saying it was only a military checkstop. No worries — they had four hours left to drive and she would be home. Fred handed the guard their papers. The guard looked suspiciously at Rachel.

"It's okay," Fred explained. "She has been pardoned by the Grand Tribunal. Her papers have the Great Dragon Seal of the Kingdom."

Those words changed everything. Within moments they were on their way with an armed soldier escorting them to ensure they safely passed the Territories.

Risking death and realizing Fred might never have this opportunity again Rachel asked,

"Fred, what do you think happens after you die?"

Fred looked astonished. He hadn't expected that question nor was he prepared to answer it. It was one he considered once but chased the question out of his mind. It was too politically incorrect. He knew even considering that question could lead him down roads he dared not walk. He motioned with his finger for Rachel to be silent — then answered, "We must not talk about such things. Go back to sleep."

Pulling over to the side of the road he turned off his surveillance recorder. Rachel was surprised but wisely didn't comment. She knew what he was doing was highly illegal but realized their conversation would be even more illegal.

"Well — I don't rightly know. What do you think happens?"

"Fred, I believe after you die you will be in an eternal place. There are only two destinations according to the Bible. We are told the road leading to life is narrow — few find it. Wide is the road leading to destruction. Your options are either Heaven, the narrow path, or Hell — the wide super highway. Most folks are on the highway to destruction."

Fred commented, "That doesn't sound appealing."

"It sounds horrible to me. Heaven is so beautiful we can't imagine it. Hell was created for the devil and his demons and is so vile and despicable you wouldn't want to imagine it."

"How do I avoid Hell?"

"Well, may I ask you some questions?"

"Sure."

"Fred, would you say you're a good person?"

"Of course. I'm giving you a ride home, aren't I?"

"Yes — very good of you. Thank you."

"My pleasure, Ma'am."

"Fred, have you ever told a lie?"

"Of course, I'd be lying if I said I hadn't."

"What does that make you?"

"A liar?"

"Have you ever stolen anything? Even something small?"

"Yes."

"And that makes you?"

"A thief I guess."

"Right again. Have you ever looked at someone lustfully?"

"Of course. I'm a man."

"Jesus said if you look at someone lustfully you've already committed adultery with them in your heart."

"Seriously?"

"Yes. Have you ever used the name of God as a cuss word?"

"Yes, all the time."

"It's called blasphemy, Fred. By your own admission — you are a lying, thieving, blaspheming, adulterer at heart. That's only four of the Ten Commandments. When you stand before God — the Righteous Judge of the universe — will you be innocent or guilty?"

"Guilty I guess."

"Heaven or Hell?"

"Hell?"

"Does that concern you?"

"Yes. Of course. Now what?"

"Fred, if you were brought before the Grand Tribunal and sentenced to death for a crime is there any way you could get out of it?"

"Never!"

"If you had a million trillion bitcoins could you purchase your freedom?"

"Never."

"Let's say a man comes into the courtroom and offers to die in your place. He offers your freedom for his death. You get to leave the courtroom. Would you be grateful?"

"Of course. Absolutely."

"Fred, that's precisely what Jesus did for you over 2000 years ago. The Bible says the wages of sin is death. You are under a death penalty from the highest court ever— a court far higher than the Grand Tribunal. Jesus, God's Son, came to earth to live and die as a man on a cruel cross — paying the debt for your sins. If you repent and believe Jesus died and rose again, you will be forgiven — born of the Spirit of God — adopted into God's forever family."

"Just repent and believe? It's that easy?"

"That easy. God made it easy so even a child could understand. You can move from death to life in a heartbeat."

"Do I just talk to Him? Will God hear me?"

"Of course. He has known you since before time began. He loves you."

Fred cried as he spoke to God for the first time in his life. He thought of the sin of his life. He had been a paid assassin and had done unspeakably horrible things.

"Jesus, thank you for what you did for me. I'm sorry for the things I've done wrong. Forgive me. Thank You I can be part of Your forever family."

"Welcome to God's family, my brother. Angels in Heaven are rejoicing over you now."

"Really? Incredible! I feel different. Like a barge load of sin that has been attached to me has been cut loose."

"That's wonderful, Fred."

"This is amazing, Rachel. I feel clean. New."

"Praise God. As you read the Bible and talk to God, He will transform you into His image. His Word is living and powerful. You'll see."

"But Bibles are forbidden. I've never seen one."

"There's one hidden at my house. I found it in Afghanistan. I'll give it to you when we get there."

"Really? Thank you."

Fred reached over and flipped on the surveillance device switch. He would have to explain the blackout time. That shouldn't be too difficult — the surveillance device seemed to be glitching a lot lately. They would understand. The Bible Rachel offered him — now that was a different matter. That could be a serious problem.

Deep Darkness

*"For, behold, darkness will cover the earth,
and thick darkness the peoples;
but Yahweh will arise on you,
and his glory shall be seen on you."
Isaiah 60:2*

MANHUNT

The morning sun cascaded through the open bedroom window. The sweet scents of jasmine and honeysuckle were on the breeze. Josh had a moment of confusion. That was strange. Wasn't it fall? Those trees flowered in the spring. All confusion vanished as Juliet gleefully bounced onto her parent's bed. Closing his eyes, Josh pretended to be asleep. Juliet loved this morning ritual. As she bounced dangerously closer — Josh leaped to life and pounced — entrapping his little girl in a giant bear hug. Juliet squealed with delight. Those giggles were a joyful sound to his ears. Josh's heart melted with love for his adorable little girl.

"Let's go sneak up on Mama," Josh whispered conspiratorially. He held his finger to his lips to warn her to be quiet. "Shhhh!" They silently slid off the bed and wedged themselves against the wall. They slid along the wall as they ever so quietly snuck up behind Mama. She was frying grits and bacon in the kitchen and pretended not to notice the ambush. Josh paused. The smell of freshly brewed coffee was tantalizing — the grits and bacon smelled heavenly.

Just as they were about to surprise Mama with a giant four-arm hug a rooster crowed. The fragrant smell of coffee dissipated into the morning mist. It was replaced by the pungent smells of the barn. Josh wanted to scream, "No! Don't go!" It was too late — they were already gone.

This couldn't be real. Maybe the barn was a bad dream? Maybe he would wake up to a precious little girl smiling at him. They would attack Mama with hugs and kisses — then have breakfast together in the sun-drenched kitchen. Josh would read from Pa's well-worn Bible. They would pray together for everything from needy neighbors to world leaders. Life would be peaceful and good.

But he wasn't home. The reality of the situation struck him and made his heart ache. He desperately missed his girls.

It was Josh's fourth day in the hayloft. There was nothing else to do — so he lay thinking about the changes in the world he had seen in the last few years.

Darkness began decades before the Rapture — when it was said the Lord's prayer was offensive. Bibles were removed from all public buildings — eventually confiscated from people's homes and burned.

After the disappearance deep darkness settled over everything—a darkness you could feel. The world was changed forever.

The king promised freedom and prosperity but instead an oppressive heaviness hung over people's lives. He told them the 'Old World Order' needed to be refurbished. National sovereignty would be a thing of the past. There would be a 'New World Order' without borders.

"The king is so wise!" the people cheered.

There was little money to help folks in need but plenty of funding for people promoting death — terrorism, abortion and euthanasia.

A year after the disappearance church doors were sealed. Killer drones and AI's were left on site to shoot anyone who even touched a sealed door.

It was against the law to talk to your child about God. If a child reported proselytizing to the authorities the parents would be removed from the home and sent to re-education camps. Strangely, those parents never returned. Politically correct parents would be brought into the home to foster and re-educate the children. It reminded some of the verse,

> *"...Children will rise up against parents,*
> *and cause them to be put to death."*
> *Mark 13:12*

World governance was controlled by the king and his elite council. His decrees were being implemented world-wide. Global studies of the environment were conducted in each of the ten earth quadrants. Many worried about global warming but the earth was getting colder — ice-storms were becoming more prevalent. Earthquakes, tidal waves, and tornadoes were an everyday occurrence.

MANHUNT

The government announced the installation of global detection software in every community. There were some questions about the Council's wisdom. Josh's little city didn't see how that would make any difference to anybody's lives. Some folks mentioned something about the Bible talking about a one-world government, but the locals reassured one another what they saw had nothing to do with that kind of thing.

High towers were put up along the roads. Some said the new technology would be invasive —that it could be a problem — that there might be higher levels of radioactivity. Again, the locals reassured one another. The government would never implement something to harm its citizens. All apprehensions simmered down.

There was talk of a new kind of technocracy — capable of monitoring the move of every person on planet earth. There would be facial recognition devices able to determine who you are from billions of files, in a fraction of a millisecond. The folks said that was too much science fiction talk.

Then the cards were introduced. These mobile mini cards were applications installed in every phone. People were told it would make life simpler. All business and monetary transactions would be made on the phone card — cash would no longer be needed. It seemed like a brilliant plan. No one could rob anyone of their credit card or bank information. It was a fool-proof system. Unhackable — until it was hacked.

Satellites would identify people's movements. Systems would be put in place to affirm or deny the basic rights to life for every citizen. It was decided the government would start rating people with an online evaluation card. This would determine who would be allowed to travel, attend school, or have the use of a plane, taxi or bus.

If you praised the government and supported their functions, you scored well. Any infringements on laws brought immediate demerits on the mini card. For example, jay walking or illegally parking brought an immediate fine — automatically deducted from your bank account. To reward good behavior you were permitted to buy groceries.

The number of points on your evaluation card determined who was allowed to live.

The people of Alabama thought this all sounded ridiculous — none of this could really happen. Folks laughed and said it was all conspiracy theories. Then the killer drones and hunting dogs were brought into every community.

The king said all nations would be drawn together, as one, to meet the common challenges and goals of mankind. He said, it would be a glorious new world order — serving an illustrious, higher purpose. He didn't tell folks the true purpose he envisioned — the world in slavery to his system.

Josh thought about how the Internet was monitored for any hint of rebellion against the king. The Network was establishing a global communications system that far surpassed any previous systems. 5G PLUS Internet was rolled out in developing countries to see if there were any issues. Some folks panicked when they heard 'The Network' generated radio frequencies harmful to humans. Because the radiation dose was going to be significantly higher with 5G PLUS, the masses were worried this would pose risks to living organisms. It was reported the radiation could cause DNA damage and lead to cancer. Many said this could cause premature aging of cells by disrupting the cells metabolism. Most folks laughed and said that was ridiculous.

The government responded by posting videos on massive TV screens in public places, telling people there was no cause for alarm. The king looked into the camera and spoke soothingly to the people. He gave glowing reports of 5G PLUS, informing the masses their messages would be able to be transmitted in less than one-millionth of a second — instant global communication. Augmented reality superimposed the king's hologram image to all cell phones. It seemed like the king was having a personal audience with each of his subjects. The majority became excited about this new technology — believing what the king told them. They hailed the king as infinitely wise.

That was the year people had to be very careful not to use banned terms like mother, father, brother, or sister. It wasn't inclusive enough — there were hundreds of gender possibilities. Grandmother and grandfather were also taboo terms. People using politically incorrect pronouns were threatened with discipline. No one knew what the discipline was — fear kept them in line.

Children were informed in schools and by the media, they didn't have to remain their biological birth sex. Children who wanted to transition were hailed as heroic. They found themselves popular and praised.

Any parents not approving of their child's gender reassignment were removed from their home. New parents would be brought into the home who would embrace the child's desire to transition. They would help the child with hormone replacement therapy and all surgical procedures. If the child wanted to change back to their birth sex, no help or support was available.

It didn't seem to register in people's minds, if everyone transitioned to the opposite sex the world would be sterile. Human life would end in one generation.

Josh thought the news from the past year was devastating. Life as it had been known on planet earth, for thousands of years, suddenly morphed into something radically different. Society became lawless — violence was the new normal.

Artificial Intelligence robots took control of every aspect of life. Their intelligence far surpassed human intelligence so most of mankind accepted their control with thankfulness. People assumed life would be easier if robots took over cleaning, childcare, teaching, and all business and financial transactions.

A new group called transhumans were developed — part human and part machine. Some were designed to provide intimate human relations. Special comfort houses were established where men could merge with seductive transhuman machines.

Some transhumans had been genetically modified in vitro — in Petri dishes and test tubes — enhancing various aspects of their physiology. Some had the DNA of a cat so had eyes that glowed and could see in the dark. The ones that had wolf DNA were still toddlers but were already presenting issues. They wanted to run with a pack and had clear terrorist tendencies. The fact that their teeth grew into sharp fangs caused a great deal of concern and trouble in the government day-cares. Horrified parents were advised to tell their wounded and traumatized children to be tolerant and inclusive.

Super soldiers were genetically engineered to be killing machines. Their capacity for love, mercy or compassion had been genetically severed. People with human DNA were becoming increasingly obsolete and unnecessary.

Some people protested against the New World Order. They disappeared. Many noticed the currents of history seemed to be flowing down a diabolical path but were helpless to do anything to stop it.

The king endorsed the commandments on the Georgia Guidestones, a huge granite monument that sits on one of the highest hills in Elbert County, Georgia. They look a lot like the stones in Stonehenge, England. Josh heard occult ceremonies and mystic celebrations were conducted there.

The engravings on the Guidestones are carved in eight different languages and offer ten guides or commandments for the world. The first commandment was the most worrisome to folks who were still able to think for themselves. The commandment stated, *"Maintain humanity under five hundred million in perpetual balance with nature."* That meant for every birth someone had to die. For earth's population to be 500,000,000, nine-tenths of the World's people would have to be eliminated. The king fully endorsed this commandment. He had plans to implement it.

The plan had several parts. There would be absolute control of the world's reproduction. People would have to apply to have a child — their DNA would be carefully screened. If someone became pregnant without a permit the child would be eliminated. Extermination of the majority of third world developing countries would be implemented as they were considered 'useless eaters'.

A new spirituality was implemented and led by the Prophet. All religions would unite as one. Anyone not participating in this union of all faiths — with worship of the king at the epicenter

— would be disciplined and given the opportunity to have their misguided thinking redirected.

Folks in town often sat on their porches in the evenings to talk about the way the world was heading. Some mockingly asked,

"Why must we believe in the virgin birth of Jesus?

"How do we know Jesus was really God?"

"Why is it necessary to believe Jesus rose from the dead?"

Josh explained to folks that heresy is choosing how much of Scripture will be believed. It is denying the nature of God and His Word. It is denying the virgin birth, the Deity of Christ, His resurrection from the dead — anything making Jesus less than God. The devil subtly led Eve to question God in the garden. When Eve entertained the question *"Has God really said...?"* the fate of mankind was sealed. Josh realized mankind was asking the same question again and was treading on very dangerous ground. He realized many who called themselves Christians no longer believed in the Deity of Christ.

Josh told folks one day Jesus Christ will rule and reign in righteousness as King of kings and Lord of lords. He will judge the living and the dead. Many refused to listen. False prophets arose saying, "If He's coming, where is He?"

"...knowing this first, that in the
last days mockers will come,
walking after their own lusts and saying,
"Where is the promise of his coming?
For, from the day that the fathers fell asleep,
all things continue as they were from
the beginning of the creation."
2 Peter 3:3,4

False prophets and teachers were in abundance in the churches. They brought in damnable heresies. Josh couldn't believe a lesbian witch was ordained as a minister in a nearby town. Hardly anyone blinked. People thought it was wonderful the church had become so inclusive and welcoming. It didn't seem to bother anyone her allegiance was not to the Kingdom of Heaven.

The Prophet told people all religions worship the same God. "How could that be true," Josh asked, "when Allah had no son. Jesus said He is the Son of God — the only way to the Father."

> *But false prophets also arose among the people,*
> *as false teachers will also be among you,*
> *who will secretly bring in destructive heresies, denying*
> *even the Master who bought them, bringing on themselves*
> *swift destruction. Many will follow their immoral ways,*
> *and as a result, the way of the truth will be maligned.*
> *2 Peter 2:1-2*

Josh found so many great books on his dad's bookshelf. He found a quote in *Colloquia Peripatetica* — written by John Duncan — a Scottish preacher who lived in the 1800s. "Christ either deceived mankind by conscious fraud, was Himself deluded and self-deceived, or He was Divine. There is no getting out of this trilemma. It is inexorable." Josh found a quote by C.S. Lewis. Lewis had shortened Duncan's quote and said, "Jesus was either a liar, a lunatic, or the Lord. Those are the only options."

Those who trusted God knew the winds of history would one day sweep away all earthly kingdoms. They knew the moments of the Antichrist kingdom would be brief and one day the King of Heaven would rule. They boldly shared their faith — they had nothing to lose. They told others Jesus promised,

> *"Behold, I stand at the door and knock.*
> *If anyone hears My voice*
> *and opens the door, then I will come in to him,*
> *and will dine with him, and he with Me."*
> *Revelation 3:20*

Many risked everything to tell others about the love of God. The days were dark but the light shone brighter.

Betrayal

"Now the brother shall betray the brother to death…"
Mark 11:12

MANHUNT

The Brotherhood withstood the horrors of Afghanistan but would it hold up to the lure of money? Josh didn't know what Tom would decide. He knew his friend needed money. Would he betray a friend? Josh argued with himself in a voice barely above a whisper.

"Tom is a loyal friend.
I've known him since childhood.
We went to school together.
He was in Afghanistan with me — not in my unit — but part of the Brotherhood.
He would never betray me.
Or would he?"

Josh lay in the hayloft debating. He desperately wanted to knock on Tom's door and ask for food and water, for medicine and a safe place to hide. But could he trust his friend? Josh argued further with himself...

"We were best men at each other's weddings.
Would the bounty on my head be too big for Tom to resist?
He's my friend.
But he desperately needs money.
But he is even closer to me than a brother.
I don't know if he would betray me."

Hunger was making Josh look longingly at food thrown to the pigs and chickens. The gator bite was infected now and incredibly sore. Moving was difficult. He didn't know what to expect as he crept down the ladder. His stomach was demanding he knock on his friend's door, but his brain was telling him that could be a fatal mistake.

He reached for the latch on the barn door and froze as he heard the latch opening from the other side. Thankfully it was dark so Josh melted back into the shadows behind the door. Tom threw a bucket of slop to his pigs and chickens.

At that moment Josh decided he wasn't ready to trust Tom. He waited to give his friend time to get back to his house before he decided to make a run for Rachel's garden. He wondered if it was safe to go there.

Thankfully, it was a cloudy night. Walking across the darkened field in the inky blackness was more difficult than he anticipated. Dizziness from not eating for days made him stumble. Josh stood swooning for a moment and steadied himself against a big ol' hemlock.

He formed a plan as he continued across the field. He would stop by Rachel's garden and see if there were any vegetables — grab a burlap sack from the shed and take anything edible he could find. He'd need it for his journey.

His plan was to head towards a place Pa had taken him as a boy. He figured it would be about a ten-hour hike. If he made it he'd be safe. The Manhunters wouldn't think to look for him there.

Josh was apprehensive as he approached his yard. Thankfully, it appeared to be abandoned. Everything looked familiar and yet had changed so much. Was it only days ago he left? How could so much have happened in such a short time?

Ma's little house on the far hill looked forlorn and empty. He was thankful Ma disappeared when so many vanished. He knew she was with the Lord — spared this nightmare. She would have been traumatized to see her little grand-sugar and her precious Rachel hauled away — horrified to know there was a Manhunt for her only son.

The animal's corrals had been busted up and his animals were gone. Stolen? Well — almost all. Boots came meowing towards him. It was a joy to see Rachel's cat. Boots looked at him like *I'm never letting you out of my sight again* — following so closely at his heels, Josh had to be careful not to trip over her.

Gathering strength, he foraged in the shed until he found a burlap sack. Someone cleaned out his shed so there was no shovel. The back door of his house was ajar. He was tempted to go in to maybe grab some clothes and search for food but didn't dare.

If squatters were in the house they wouldn't be at all pleased to see him.

Digging in the soft dirt with his bare hands felt good. Rachel had dug there.

"God, please be with my girls."

Boots followed as he foraged for all the food he could find. There were a few beets and potatoes — a cabbage was lying off to the side like it had been dropped there on purpose.

"Thank you, Rachel," Josh whispered as he dropped the vegetables into the sack.

The raw potato was like a feast — Josh devoured it. He offered Boots a piece but she sniffed it disdainfully. She must have been dining on fat mice.

"At least I have part of my family." Josh smiled as he scratched Boots behind her torn ear.

They headed for the only place in Alabama Josh felt would be safe.

"It looks like it's from Middle Earth," Josh told Boots. "I thought my Pa was the coolest dad ever for bringing me on a camping trip to Dismals Canyon. I was about twelve at the time."

Josh put Boots on his shoulder.

"It's in northwest Alabama. Pa said it could easily have been in Tolkien's *Lord of the Rings*. It's one of the most fascinating places I've seen. The canyons are full of sandstone caves, waterfalls, and natural bridges. There's giant moss-covered boulders strewn about by ancient earthquakes and floods. It's an eighty-five-acre natural conservatory. It's the perfect place to hide. No one will look for us there."

Josh realized it would be a challenge to travel ten hours and not be noticed. The new plan was pretty basic. Follow Highway 43 south and stay out of sight. Thankfully, much of the terrain was covered with trees.

His Marine training helped. Josh was good at hiding. He passed the communities of Tuscumbia, Littleville, and Russelville with no issues. For some unknown reason the drones seemed to have been called away. They usually patrolled the highways.

Even the AI police were nowhere to be seen. The glitches were definitely working in his favor.

After what seemed like an eternity of walking, they reached Dismals Canyon.

"Well, Boots. Scottish-Irish settlers came to this place about a century before. I heard there's a beautiful place in Scotland called "Dismals" so the name fit this canyon."

It took hours to hike to the canyon floor. They followed a trail through Dismal Branch — past massive boulders that seemed to reach the sky. Waterfalls thundered as they cascaded down cliffs.

Giant timber stands watched like silent sentinels over the canyon. Hemlock, sweetgum, oak, tulip poplar, beech, and magnolia were surrounded by soft green ferns. Josh was sure it was the most breathtakingly beautiful place on earth — next to his farm, that is.

"Pa told me that back in the early 1800's, U.S. troops rounded up the native Americans in the area and held them like cattle for weeks — in these very canyons and caves. Can you imagine? Pa said the Chickasaw people were driven like animals to Muscle Shoals. They trudged along what has since been called The Trail of Tears."

Josh imagined he could hear the weeping of the people in the wind sighing through the trees.

"Pa and I camped in a big old cave called Temple Cave. It will make an excellent hideout. We can build a campfire there and not be noticed. There's a waterfall right outside the entrance to the cave so we can have drinking water and a shower. What more could a man and his cat ask for?"

Boots jumped off his shoulder to search the cave for mice.

"Boots, just you wait. At twilight we'll have 'night-lights' — billions of "dismalites". They are also called glow-worms. They make a soft, iridescent light on the walls of the cave."

Boots found the critters fascinating.

Josh found a paleo spear point in a grotto and attached it to a sturdy branch. He used it to hunt rabbits. Thankfully he still had his pocketknife. It was one of the last things he had from his

Pa so he wasn't about to leave it in the gator's eye. Boots loved roast rabbit.

Josh carried a pole covered in pitch and fire to keep the mountain lions away. Marine wilderness survival training was paying off once again.

Josh lost all track of time. Days turned into weeks as he lived a Robinson Crusoe existence. One night, as Josh stared at the beautiful night sky, he could see why King David once looked in awe at a similar sky and proclaimed,

> *"The Heavens declare the glory of God.*
> *The expanse shows his handiwork."*
> *Psalm 19:1*

The stars looked like diamonds strewn over a black velvet cloth. Josh wondered if King David marveled at the sky from a similar cave as he hid from King Saul. David was also the prey of a manhunt. He was also falsely accused.

Josh had been putting a hot knife on the gator bite to stave off infection. It had been working — until today. The wound was festering red — warm and swollen. Who knows what the gator was carrying? Without antibiotics Josh realized he would soon be dead. He knew his kidneys couldn't handle the infection and his vital organs would shut down within seventy-two hours.

He had to get help soon. Tom was his only hope, but nagging questions remained...

"Will Tom betray me to death?
Will his loyalty to the Brotherhood remain?
We vowed to stand together unto death.
Will his oath stand this trial?"

Josh squeezed his eyes shut, hoping when he opened them again, he would wake up from this nightmare. It didn't work.

The hike back to Sheffield had been grueling — it rained both days and nights. He shivered — unable to get warm. The wounds looked angry — festering. He had a fever and was beginning to get delirious.

Josh realized it was time to ask Tom for help. He tried to climb down the ladder but couldn't keep his balance — he was too dizzy. The hayloft seemed to be spinning. He lay down determined to talk to Tom in the morning.

When Josh opened his eyes again it was pitch dark — probably the middle of the night. A bright light flashed directly in his face. Josh recoiled in pain and confusion from the blinding light.

A gruff voice demanded,
"What are ya' doin' in my barn?"
Was that Tom? Josh was shocked to hear his friend sound so angry. He realized he was probably unrecognizable. His beard had grown. He hadn't washed for days — since the waterfall at Dismals Canyon. His clothes were muddy and ragged.

That's when he noticed the gun.
He called out, "Tom. It's me. Josh."
Josh was totally unprepared for the reply.
"I know who you are. Why are you here?"
Josh was confused.
"It's me, Tom."
"I said I know. Why didja' think you could come here and hole up in my barn? I heard you're wanted by the Manhunters."
Josh froze. This wasn't a nightmare.
Breathe. Breathe.
He had to think calmly. He was in Tom's hayloft and Tom was pointing a gun at him. There had to be a misunderstanding.
"Tom, it's me. Joshua Williams."
Josh was getting desperate.
"I said I know! You're are a dangerous criminal! It's all over the news!"
Breathe, Josh. Steady. Don't' panic.
"But I didn't do anything, Tom. It's all a mistake. I don't know what's going on."

Tom lowered the flashlight. Maybe that was a good sign? As Josh became accustomed to the darkness, he was shocked to see Tom. He barely recognized his friend.

His face was lined with worry. He looked haggard — much older than his thirty-five years.

His eyes were wild — like a caged animal's. His hair was matted and his clothes were torn and dirty. Tom's cheeks were hollow and his face looked gaunt. There were dark circles under his eyes. Barely anything about his friend was recognizable — just his voice.

"Tom, are you okay? What's happened?"

The hand holding the gun was trembling. Josh tried to get up. Tom barked, "Don't move!"

Josh lay on the hay praying for strength and for God to snap Tom out of whatever this mood was. Tom seemed to be deciding on something. Finally, he spat out,

"Get up. Let's go to the house."

Josh heard tell the road to a friend's house is never long. He found that to be a lie.

Tom walked behind him, pointing the gun and the flashlight at his back.

This can't be happening. Tom is my friend. We grew up together...

Once in the kitchen, Tom used belts to tie Josh to a chair.

His voice spewed acid as he snarled, "Why did ya kill them?"

"Kill who, Tom?"

"Right, Mr. Innocent. You know darned well who. Rachel and Juliet."

Josh felt like a mule kicked him in the stomach. He felt the PTSD gaining strength. He was in complete shock.

Breathe, Josh. It's okay. You will be okay. God, help me.

"What do you mean, Tom?'

"Stop playing me for a fool. The Manhunters will want to know where you hid the bodies."

Josh felt numb. He could barely think.

"I don't know what you're talkin' about, Tom."

"Liar!"

"Honest, Tom. The Manhunters took them away. I watched them."

Anger boiled up in Tom as he shouted, "You're are a liar, Josh! I don't know how I was ever fooled into thinkin' you were my friend. I looked up to you — you're nuthin' but a lyin', thievin', murderer — pretending to be a godly man!"

"I didn't kill anyone, Tom. You know me."

"I know you all right. You're nuthin' but a lyin' hypocrite."

"Tom, what about the oath we made. Brothers always."

"You broke that vow yourself, Josh. I don't keep vows with murderers."

"But I didn't murder anyone."

"I can't believe I trusted you. You're gonna pay for your ways."

He pleaded with Tom to listen to reason.

He may as well have pleaded with a wall.

Josh was sure this was a nightmare he would wake up from soon.

"Tom, you're makin' a huge mistake."

"Nope. No mistake."

Josh watched in disbelief as Tom picked up his phone.

"Tom, don't do this! Please!"

"Shut up."

"Please..."

"Hello, I need the county Manhunters Division. I wanna' claim a bounty..."

About the Author

Rena is a mother, artist, writer, and coffee lover. She has taught Kindergarten to Grade 12 in various settings in Canada and China.

Rena has discovered writing can be an addictive adventure. She has written *A Life Set Free*, *Mommy & Baby's Journal*, *Bubs Bunny Goes to Camp*, *The Narrow Path Trilogy* and is amassing scribbly notes for *Beyond Betrayal*.

God has given Rena incredible opportunities to be involved in short-term missions around the globe as an Ambassador with the Department of Eternal Affairs. She believes nothing is impossible when our lives are surrendered to God. She sincerely hopes to meet you in Heaven. Please read the next page for your personal invitation.

Blog — renagroot.com

Dear Friend,

If you aren't a Christian — what's stopping you? Call on the Name of the LORD Jesus Christ and you will be saved. Life is fragile. You have no way of knowing if this will be your last invitation to be born into a Kingdom that cannot be shaken. If you would like to commit your life to Jesus Christ here is a prayer you can pray to Him or please use your own words:

"Lord Jesus,
I am sorry I have hardened my heart against You
and refused to believe You are the Messiah.
I repent (am sorry) for all my sins. Please forgive
me and cleanse me from all unrighteousness.
Create in me a clean heart.
I believe You are the Son of God and that You died
on the cross in my place to pay my sin debt.
Thank You that Your blood was shed
for me so I could be forgiven.

Yours is the only Name in Heaven or on
Earth by which mankind can be saved.
Please come into my heart, come into my life, fill
me with Your Holy Spirit. I realize in my own
strength I can do nothing. Thank You that I am not
saved because of anything good I have done. I am
saved because of Your love, grace, and mercy.
Thank You that my name is written in Your Book of Life.
Please lead me by Your Holy Spirit as I
walk Earth's perilous final days.

Thank You, Lord Jesus.
I ask this in Your Mighty Name!"

Photo Credits

The Rebellion
Photo by Ramazan-tokay from Unsplash
https://unsplash.com/photos/_Lwd3fe5DqI

Manhunt
Image by Stocksnap from Pixabay
https://pixabay.com/photos/dark-nature-trees-plant-fog-cold-2586359/

Broken Dreams
Image by StockSnap from Pixabay
https://pixabay.com/photos/guy-man-people-dark-shadow-hands-2617866/

Rachel
Photo by JacksonDavid from Pixababy
https://pixabay.com/photos/freedom-girl-travel-adventure-4782870/

News
Photo by Jon Tyson from Unsplash
https://unsplash.com/photos/XmMsdtiGSfo

Where Were You, God?
Photo by Mysticartdesign from Pixabay
https://pixabay.com/photos/walk-landscape-trees-sun-sky-man-445272/

The Pit
Photo by Ian Chen from Unsplash
https://unsplash.com/photos/wrrgZwI7qOY

Sweet Home, Alabama
Photo by Caroline Hernandez from Unsplash
https://unsplash.com/photos/5BKUtjC7O6A

The Witnesses
https://pixabay.com/photos/fantasy-light-mood-sky-beautiful-2861107/

The Children's Prison
Photo by Yandso1 from Pixabay
https://pixabay.com/photos/people-human-child-portrait- 2833090/

Sheep Among Wolves
Photo by Glen Carstens-Peters from Unsplash
https://unsplash.com/photos/F-u9hLx19uY

Love Not Your Life Unto Death
Photo by Prateek Gautam
https://unsplash.com/photos/wX1GSlEHzuc

Released
Photo by Jill Wellington
https://pixabay.com/photos/woman-happiness-sunrise-silhouette-570883/

Dispatch from the Grand Tribunal - The Great Dragon Seal of the Kingdom
Pixabay-Coffee
https://pixabay.com/vectors/circle-icons-dragon-ring-snake-1295218/

MANHUNT

Deep Darkness
Image by StockSnap from Pixabay
https://pixabay.com/photos/people-man-walking-alone-dark-2567788/

Betrayal
Photo by StockSnap from Pixababy
https://pixabay.com/photos/black-and-white-people-man-alone-2603103/

'About the Author' photo was taken by a forever friend on Rena's last night in Tianjin, China

Manufactured by Amazon.ca
Bolton, ON